The Nine Lives of Tigger Digger

MARGARET GRANT

Illustrations by Gordon Grant

PUBLISHED BY
MYNYDD LLWYDIARTH PRESS

Dear Leo,
Always allow your compassion to shine. Blessings, love & light.
Margaret Grant. Dec. 2019

All human characters in this book are fictitious and
any resemblance to actual persons living or dead
is entirely coincidental. However, the animals in the story are
based on real creatures, owned or encountered by the author.

More information about Margaret Grant can be found at:
margaretgrantauthor.wordpress.com

Front cover and jacket design by
Kertu Laur of Sarafista Designs

Illustrations by Gordon Grant

Published by Mynydd Llwydiarth Press 2020
ISBN 978-0-9930463-2-2 paperback
ISBN 978-0-9930463-3-9 ebook Kindle

To the wonderful pets
that have enriched our family life
so incredibly, with their loyalty
and total, comforting love.

Readers may like to discuss each chapter with an adult as they go along. You will find some interesting discussion questions for each chapter at the back of the book.

Contents

CHAPTER 1

THE BAGGED PUSS

The smell of hessian sack was stifling. Once the rough sack, quick as a wink, had been popped over my head encasing my entire body, I sneezed and gasped. My squashed whiskers twitched and I panicked. My claws raked desperately, trying to rip their way out; but I could do nothing. My claws were now enmeshed and entangled in the dreaded weave of the sack.

I felt myself being lifted onto something like a couch. Then suddenly, I heard the thump of a door banging shut and an engine roaring into life. I was being transported somehow -

trundling along at break-neck speed. I tried to keep still, but was being jostled and tumbled about; just like the clothes I loved to watch in Nan Knitwarm's kitchen, as they spun around in her clothes drier making that whooshing noise. The memory of it made my nose trace circles in the air. But now my head began to spin dizzily and I felt very sick. I began yowling.... the loudest yowl I could yowl. I knew that my tormentor would witness my vomiting if I were not soon released.

Just in time to save my pride, the vehicle jolted to a halt and a Human Bean, smelling a great deal of old sausage and fried black pudding, lifted me like a bad smell and dropped me out of the sack onto a muddy lane. 'Scram!' he shouted. And scram I did.

For a moment I was terrified, crouching behind the trunk of a nearby tree. It didn't surprise me in the least that my tormentor.... grim-faced 'Noddle of a Nephew Newton' could be so cruel. He was always banging at Nan Knitwarm's door begging for more money to bet on the horses. I cowered and crouched even lower as I heard his van engine roar again. It sped away, taking with it some of my terror.

I wasn't too sure where I had been dumped, but it was such a relief to breathe real air.... fresh air from the moors. In contrast to the tainted smells of the suburban streets where I had lived, these new smells seemed truly wonderful. Before me was a muddy lane, where recent rain had collected in glorious drinking puddles. I lapped at one. Like magic the cool, fresh water helped the awful scratchiness in my throat to disappear.

The sky was open and bright blue now.... only a distant cloud remembered it had rained. A patchwork of fields and copses of trees stretched out as far as my eyes could see and, through a five-barred, wooden gate, I could see below me a vast valley. It held the exciting, dazzling expanse of what I would come to know as a *reservoir*. It was like a great lake of water where Human Beans collected the rain and the streams. I supposed they saved the water for a non rainy day.... a very big puddle indeed!

My relief at finding I could move and breathe soon turned to wibble-wobble worry. The sun was beginning to go down and I knew it would turn cold and I would need somewhere dry and warm to sleep. I was hungry too. No meat now from a fragrant smelling bowl on Nan Knitwarm's kitchen floor.

I wondered what had happened to

her - my favourite Human Bean? Ron the postman was a frequent visitor to her humble terraced house, as Nan always had a brew ready for him half way through his deliveries. I liked Ron. He understood cats and never dared to disturb me from my favourite cushion on one of Nan's kitchen chairs. Instead, he would give my chin a rub and scratch between my ears as he sipped his tea and checked that Nan was allright.

The day things went horribly wrong I woke Nan as usual by creeping up on the bed and nudging her bulbous nose. She always snorted and turned over for a while, cradling me warm against her fleecy nightdress and telling me how handsome and wonderful I was. You have to keep at it with these Human Beans. They don't wake up easily and can be quite lazy about getting up at dawn when you are in need of a feed and a trip outside to 'water' the garden.

I knew the best tactic was to persist in licking her cheek or her double chin and purr loudly into her ear. I had been known to knock things off her dressing table accidentally-on-purpose to get her out of bed, but then she would get cross with me and put me out without any breakfast!

All seemed to be going my way. She grunted and got out of bed, shuffled her way to the bathroom whilst I waited politely outside. Then she nearly tripped over me on the way out. She had forgotten to put on her spectacles!

I sat at the top of the stairs, waiting for her to dress quickly as it was a chilly morning and then I raced ahead of her downstairs and into the kitchen, indicating that she should follow and feed me.

She responded very well and hurried along, opening a sachet of my favourite chicken dish before she had even put on the kettle for herself. All was going well. By the time I was ready to sit on a cushion next to her and groom myself clean whilst she ate her breakfast, she was humming a tune and planning her day.

'I think I'll go to the park and feed the ducks and then I will pop into the Co-op to get some of our favourite foods. We shall have a little treat today, Tigger Digger,' she crooned to me. 'What would you say to some tuna, my lad? Shall we indulge?' We were always *indulging* and that was the way I liked it. I was well fed and as a result had a glossy striped coat, a neat set of four white paws and a silky white throat and stomach. Nan was well fed too, but I think her taste in chocolate biscuits and crisps was her downfall. She was an overweight egg shape and quite 'doddery on her pins'. (I had heard a neighbour say this about her. I think it meant 'unsteady'.)

She began clearing the breakfast dishes and I sat next to the kitchen door and stared at her a while, indicating it was time for her to let me out into her tiny garden. I could tell she wasn't thinking of me. She was thinking of how she needed to get back upstairs and find her spectacles. She turned quickly to get them and fell over the kitchen rug, landing splat on the hard floor.

By the time Ron the Postie had arrived for his morning 'cuppa', I was desperate.... desperate to wake up Nan, desperate to 'water' the garden and desperately frightened. Ron saw me pawing and mewing at the kitchen window and tried to get in through the door, but it was locked.

Ron knew where Nan Knitwarm hid her spare key from her 'Noddle Nephew Newton.' It was under my drinking dish outside. Ron said that Newton was named after a famous physicist called Isaac Newton, who discovered the law of gravity and other important things.... but he also said that just because one was named after an intelligent person didn't necessarily mean you were intelligent. I wondered what he meant? Maybe 'Noddle Newton' was a nickname and not Nan's nephew's real name?

As soon as the door creaked open, I sped out of the kitchen door to do the necessary in the garden. Ron shouted at Nan to try to wake her up, but he had little success. I heard her give just a small groan of pain and then Ron calling for an ambulance.

I recognised the word 'ambulance' immediately. It meant a lot of siren noise, a blue flashing light and screechy tyres from a large, white and yellow vehicle almost as big as a small bus. I am ashamed to say that, although I cared about Nan Knitwarm, I fled and hid behind next door's wheelie bins until the beast had driven away with Nan inside it on a carry bed. I wasn't quite sure what to do. I had never met this sort of situation before. I hadn't finished my breakfast, so I supposed I would have to go begging from other cat owners.

Human Beans can be very gracious and offer you the odd tit-bit if you look prettily at them and wind around their legs affectionately. Although I have to say the first time I tried this on with Nan's nephew Newton, he kicked me across the room.

As luck would have it, Mrs. Benchsit across the street from Nan's house was hanging out her washing and had seen Nan depart.

'Whisked her away to hospital have they, my love? And who will look after you? My Jack Russell will have you for his dinner if I let you in my house. You can have some bacon scraps for now outside your back door until that Newton character makes an appearance.' She sniffed and, carrying her empty wash basket on her hip, disappeared inside to get me my scraps.

I think the proper way of saying 'Human Beans' is 'human beings.' But I like to think individually. I see an egg-shaped glow around most people and it makes them look bean shaped.... so 'Human Beans' they are to me. Some have warm glows about them, some frosty, some angry, some grumpy and some twinkly. Mrs. Benchsit had a warm glow around her bean shape and I felt I could trust her. However, I was disappointed that she had a yapping,

Jack Russell dog to fuss about instead of fussing me. True to her promise, though, she came outside again with a saucer of scraps. The saucer had a picture of the queen on it, so I felt very honoured indeed.

Feeling honoured did not last long. Newton had heard on the grapevine - (Whatever that is? I think it must be a new kind of mobile phone) - that Nan would be gone for a while and that her house would be empty. I watched him suspiciously as he tried the door, but it did not have Nan's usual chain across and he put his shoulder to it and crashed his way in. I stupidly followed him to see what he was going to get up to.... Big mistake! He rampaged through the house looking for money, turning things upside down, throwing the contents of drawers onto the floor and generally having a bad tantrum about not finding any money. Of course there wasn't any money. It was her pension day today and she had not been to get it from the post office before she fell.

'Argh! Drat it. Cat it.... no money for the gee-gees. I will just have to sell a little jewellery to bump up the funds.' With that he pocketed Nan's gold retirement watch.... the one she wore only for special occasions. Things were going from bad to worse. Policemen do not understand cat language, or I would have been a good witness in court, I considered sadly.

When I thought things could not get any worse Newton spotted me witnessing his every move and made a grab for me. I'm pretty agile and sprang around the living room, leading him a merry dance around the coffee table, behind the television and up and down the stairs. He reminded me of a spider dodging about on a slippery, icy roof. He eventually cornered me behind the sofa and got me in that dreaded sack.

'Gotcha, Tigger Digger!' he announced as he pounced.

Being out on the moors was splendid in fine weather, but come dark it would go very cold. Something in my nose and whiskers told me to search for the smell of hay. I think it was my ***INKSTINK*** telling me what to do. Human Beans call it 'instinct'.... the sort of knowing that you just know. Somewhere in your brain it is like a letter someone has sent in huge capital letters written in **very black ink**.... something that you cannot possibly ignore!

A distant memory of my mother carrying me to safety just after I had been born came to mind. She had gently put me down in a nest of new hay and licked me clean, before encouraging me to suckle her milk along with my sisters and brothers. It was a long-ago memory, fading in and out, but the smell of the hay was the biggest part of the memory. I would be safe if I found hay.

My nose and whiskers called me to a big building beyond a five-barred, iron gate set into a stone wall. I could smell the hay inside from yards away;

but danger most terrible lurked in the farmyard.

Chained to the farmhouse wall on a path to this barn was a snarling, growling sheepdog. I had met his breed before, but never one so vicious looking. He bared his teeth and stared at me evilly. He sent a message to my *inkstink* saying he would rip me apart if he got anywhere near me. He began barking so loudly that my ears hurt like the pricking jabs of Nan Knitwarm's knitting needles.

However, beyond the pain I could just hear the chirrup of a robin hopping along the top of the wall. *Inkstink* told me he was looking for worms and I decided to follow him stealthily. He made his way to a wooden fence and then around the back of the barn to peck red, wiggly things from a muck pile. I thanked him for guiding me. He was using message pictures sent to my inner eye.... I think Human Beans would call it 'telepathy'. I felt safer now that the barn building stood between the ravening dog and myself.

He was barking really furiously by this time, so I knew I would have to hide.... I teetered for a moment on the wooden fence and then dropped down with a thud into the mud, my white paws suddenly sticky and black. I squelched for a few steps, then dodged underneath a plastic water trough outside the side of the barn and crouched low. The barking had alerted the farmer and she came out of her door brandishing a torch and holding a plate of fragrant food.

'What are you telling me, Spud? Have we got poachers again? Is someone trying to steal our sheep or our stone-walling? Maybe some idiot is planning to burn out a stolen car in the lane? Or maybe a fox is after my hens, eh?'

Spud, the sheepdog, calmed and became more interested in the food the farmer set down for him before she scoured the buildings with her torch. I could feel my heart pounding as her torchlight suddenly settled on the water trough.

'Mmm! Cat paw-prints in the mud.

You ruffian, Spud! It's only a stray cat. One more ratter in the barn will not harm. Stop fussing and eat your dinner,' she soothed as she turned her back on me, shivered with the new cold of the evening and went hastily back indoors. I caught a glimpse of a log fire through the farmhouse door and longed for heat as well as food.

I found that I could just squeeze under the corrugated, metal wall of the barn and into the huge building with its towers of hay. It smelled wonderful. I clawed my way to the top of a bale and sank my backside into the warmth of the hay.

'You will have to do better than that if you want to keep your ears!' prrped a voice from below. A huge fat, black and white cat stared at me with his yellow eyes from a pile of loose hay below. His ears were a very weird shape.... not pointed like that of a normal cat, but C shaped. I did not like to comment on them, as it might have appeared rude.... We cats have such delicate codes of politeness. However, he announced, 'I'm

Chip. I am the only cat allowed into the farmhouse.... as long as I keep down the mice. I suppose you are wondering whatever happened to my ears?'

'The thought did cross my mind,' I said timidly. 'I have never seen such a special set of ears before.'

'I was stupid enough to sleep out in this barn during a very frosty spell and forgot to bury my ears in the hay. The tips of my ears had frozen solid whilst I slept and fell off the next day. You should never fall asleep in the winter without covering your whole body. You might wake up with a bit missing if you get careless.'

'Good advice! I will remember that in future. My name is Tigger, by the way. You don't happen to know where I could get some food do you? Does the farmer feed the cats in the barn?'

'You'll be lucky. Farmer Parkin invites me in and always feeds me at least twice a day. But the barn cats she leaves to fend for themselves so that they will keep down the rat and mice population.

You do know how to catch rats and mice I suppose?'

'I did once catch a rat near our dustbins, but it was only small. My mother gave me one or two lessons I vaguely remember, but I'm not that brilliant at it.'

'It will be fully dark soon and the barn cats will begin stalking and crouching, listening for the rats and mice who come in here to nest. They will not want you around to spoil their hunt. You had better stick with me. They will not attack you if you are with me.'

'I have not greeted them yet, but I can smell this is their territory and I would not like to get into a fight, so I will stay close to you if you don't mind. However, I'm really frightened of the sheepdog. I keep thinking he will eat me alive if he gets hold of me.'

'Wise not to get too near him until I have introduced you properly. He is a pussycat really. Loves being stroked and petted, but knows he must guard the house and livestock. I feel sorry for him.... that chain must be so irksome. As soon as he recognizes you as a friend he will not be so fierce.'

'Thank you for being so friendly! I am used to other cats being very territorial.... hissing and growling, defending their own patch of land very strongly. I have never had a cat friend before.'

'There is always a first time for everything young chap. There is plenty of territory to share up here on the moors,' Chip replied. 'I suppose you are from somewhere crowded?'

'I lived with Nan Knitwarm in a suburban street with lots of cars to dodge and small gardens to dig in. That is until Noddle Nephew Newton decided to catnap me and dump me on the lane. Everywhere here seems so vast.'

'We are indeed fortunate to have so much freedom to roam up here,' purred Chip contentedly. 'Ours is a wonderful kingdom which stretches for miles and miles .... and miles.'

Sooooo.... began the second chapter of my life. I was soon introduced to Spud the sheepdog. Once Chip had convinced him that I wasn't a threat, day upon day he became a more familiar and more trusted friend. He always watched out for danger and whenever the gang of wild cats, Bumfleas, Glumteaser, Gobblechops, Yarlminger and Clawit threatened to attack me, he would set up his snarling and barking and I would run and hide behind him. I admit I was not much of a tiger when it came to being brave. I am not sure why Nan Knitwarm named me Tigger. Maybe it was my stripey coat that reminded her of a tiger.

It saddened me a great deal that I no longer had a knee to care for, nor a hand to stroke me. Feeling unloved is not a happy way to live. If it wasn't for Chip and now Spud, my days would be entirely miserable and lonely.

Team hunting with Chip became a daily game of fun for him, but was vital to me for food. However, I did begin to lose weight and, with only the rodents to catch for my dinner, I soon began to show my ribs, with worms in my stomach and fleas on my fur.... generously donated by the rats and mice that we had caught.

Occasionally Chip would encourage me to share some scraps, which Farmer Parkin put out for him. They were a welcome, tasty treat. But, to be honest, I wasn't very good at hunting. My pounce lacked bounce Chip declared.

CHAPTER 2

TRAPPED

The first snow of the year had started to make an appearance and Farmer Parkin worked very hard getting hay and nutfeed to her sheep. She took into the barn any ewes that looked as though they might birth a lamb very early. Life was much harder for me too, as Bumfleas, Glumteaser, Gobblechops, Yarlminger and Clawit now took over the top of the hayloft and slept there continuously. It meant I had to squeeze into a miserable, cold corner or hide under the water trough. Chip encouraged me to snuggle up to a sheep, but I soon found the sheep weren't keen. They were frightened that I would hurt their lambs. During these bitterly cold days I saw less and less of Chip as he preferred to stay indoors by the fire. Lucky chap!

As I grew thinner it became harder to keep warm, especially as my food was only what I could catch with the occasional lick of Spud's empty plate. 'You are welcome to share my kennel,' he surprised me by saying on the coldest day I ever remember. Inside his wooden doghouse he had a thick pile of hay and a blanket to sit on. I thanked him and squeezed in next to him.

'I don't want your fleas!' he grumbled, 'So I hope my flea powder works as well for cat fleas as dog fleas!'

'I have no way of knowing if it does. Nan Knitwarm used to squeeze a little bit of liquid on the back of my neck to keep all those things at bay. I must admit to being very itchy these days. I miss being groomed. My coat is becoming as scratchy as straw and I do not enjoy cleaning myself any more.'

'Sad times,' said Spud, giving me an

affectionate lick on my nose.

The snow came thicker and life harder for everyone up on the moors. Farmer Parkin was well prepared for being snowed-in and had stocks of food in her freezer in an old outhouse. She had a monster of a four-wheel drive vehicle to help her check on her sheep and a tractor with a snowplough on the front to help clear the lanes.

One crisp morning she had been out snow clearing at the top of a nearby hill when I realised that she had created great walls of snow taller than people by the sides of the lane. The drystone walls that normally edged the fields had completely disappeared under her snow walls, but the wrens that had built their nests in them still needed to get out for food and had created tunnels in the snow so that they could breathe and feed.

A pair of them was out in the middle of the lane pecking at nutfeed that had fallen off the back of her trailer. I resisted *inkstink* to pounce on them for food. I couldn't help admiring them.... such small creatures with such huge daring! They darted back into their snow tunnels as I padded up the lane towards them. How I wished I were as courageous.

My curiosity was tickling my whiskers and driving me to find out where Farmer Parkin kept her sheep. I followed behind the tractor's trailer towards a field a good distance away. It had holly bushes in it for the sheep to graze upon; but she had spread a feast of what Chip told me were turnips onto the field. She was also busy sprinkling a fine layer of silage on top of the snow, which kept her flock busily grazing. A wood of beech, birch and pine trees at the top of the hill kept the sheep sheltered from the biting winds. So here they huddled together to keep warm, chomping away. Ohhhh! I was soooo hungry!

I sniffed at a turnip but it did not smell as though I could eat it. I sniffed at the sheep nuts and tried a little bite, but they tasted of sawdust. I tried licking a holly bush, but although the snow on them gave me water, the prickles to my nose were not worth the bother. Sheep feed was no good for cats!

Inkstink told me that I had better head for the woodland so that I could shelter from a coming snowstorm. If my nose were correct it would soon be howling around me. For now it was so quiet in the woodland, warmer too as the trees spread their friendly security blanket of radiating heat around me. Where could I curl up against the coming blizzard? Could I roost in a tree like the woodpigeons? No! Bad idea! I would probably freeze and fall off my perch.

However, my 'search it and find it' sensor led me at last to a brown-painted waggon. It had a curved roof, a sliding door and nestled amongst the trees like a hibernating hedgehog. Good! The door was open and inside I could see that someone had dumped an old car seat. That would do very well as a temporary snuggle spot. I curled up against the peeling leather of the seat and tucked my head underneath my paws. I curled my tail tightly around my nose and tried to drift off to sleep, as the fresh snow and wind began hurtling at the landscape. I was reminded of Chip's warning about bits dropping off in the frost.

The wind sang in the trees around my shelter and the snow began to drive horizontally and deepened alarmingly. Luckily the wheels of my waggon lifted me several feet above ground level and I had plenty of snow in the open doorway to lick if I needed water. The snow soon covered my paw tracks and I felt cocooned from danger. I drifted into nose-twitching Dreamland, relaxed and imagined it was summer.

I jumped as a loud bang shook the waggon. At first I had felt its gentle rock in the wind, but now the gale had violently shaken the whole structure. The sliding door had suddenly slid. I was shut in. I was trapped. I felt weak and dizzy and very frightened. I began to yowl and claw at the door, hoping I could make it slide open, but with every claw and every scratch I grew weaker and my voice became little more than a squeak. I needed to think clearly. I needed to stop clawing and panicking.

A tiny crack at the bottom of the door told me it was still daylight. Maybe if I yowled loudly enough, Farmer Parkin would hear me. I licked a trickle of melting snow from the inside of the door and began trying out my voice once more; but with the wind screeching louder than ever I began to give up hope of being rescued. Suddenly I heard the noise of the tractor engine starting up. Oh! No! Farmer Parkin was heading back to the safety of the farmhouse and definitely leaving me behind.

I am not sure how many days and nights I was locked in that dreadful prison. I had given up hope of escape and convinced myself I would perish without food. I still had water; for as the snow melted it trickled and dripped from an icicle developing from a hole in the roof. I tried reaching out to my friends, Chip and Spud. Maybe through *inkstink*

or telepathy I could link up with their minds. Perhaps they would be worried about me and *inkstink* would tell them where to come and find me. The damp and the cold were eating into my bones and my fur was frozen into spikes all around my body. I waited for the Light of Heaven to take me away. I remember my mother telling me about how it came to accompany you at the end of your life, after all your nine lives had been spent. It didn't seem fair that I had only spent two so far.

I stirred from Dreamland on the most peculiar of days. I heard boots scrunching on frosty snow. I could see bright sunshine filtering through the crack in the base of the door and blue sky through the pinprick of a hole in the roof. I could smell old sausage and fried black pudding! Oh No! Noddle Nephew Newton!

I prayed to the bright light that I would have nine lives and not only two. I had been bagged and dumped, trapped and starved. Who knew what danger was in store for me now?

I dragged myself fearfully behind the car seat and waited. Then Newton slid back the heavy sliding door and hitched his backside onto the floor of the waggon. As luck would have it, he did not even look around inside. He was more intent on staring through a pair of eyenoculars. Hiding his body behind the inside wall of the waggon, he strained around to the outside with the eyenoculars, focussing on a huge stone house on the other side of the lane.

Once it had had handsome, Georgian windows, but they were rotting now. At the beginning of its drive it also sported a very imposing set of stone pillars, housing rusty, black and gold iron gates. I remembered Chip's telling me about this very grand house. It used to belong to a very wealthy landowner. Then it passed to a less wealthy family called the Bimblewicks, who allowed the whole place to fall into disrepair.

'He's looking for a way in to burgle the house,' I thought. 'And maybe he doesn't see very well either, so needs eyenoculars to look through?'

'Ha! Late risers,' Newton said to himself. 'They've only just put on their fire to start cooking breakfast and it's already ten o' clock!' Newton adjusted the eyenoculars and stared again at Bimblewick House, watching a curl of smoke rise from the kitchen chimney. I peeped around the car seat and noticed a silver-haired lady opening the kitchen blinds.

I thought I had better make my escape whilst he was still preoccupied with the morning eating habits of the Bimblewicks. I slipped out from behind the car seat. However, I froze for a moment when I heard the excited noise of children playing in the snow in the distance. It reminded me of how the children in Nan Knitwarm's street used to throw stones at me and I gulped in sheer terror.

I didn't dare breathe. I steeled myself; then in slow motion silently lowered myself to the ground and around the corner of the waggon. I could hear the laughter of the children on the other side of the wood. Thankfully the ground was so crisp that my paw prints were hardly noticeable. However, just in case, I hid behind a waggon wheel and waited until Newton left.

He had parked his van out of immediate sight, around a bend in the lane. I wondered fearfully when he would return to burgle the Bimblewicks and how I might help them. As my paw steps slowed and weakened, I realised that I was in no fit state to help anyone. I must get back to Spud and ask his advice.

It took me a good while to drag myself down the lane and back to the farmhouse. Spud saw me as I crept under the main gate and yelped and whined, wagging his tail in greeting when he saw me.

'What a state you are in! Where have you been? We thought you had been bag-napped again. Chip was certain you were trapped and starving, but he has been ill and kept indoors, so could not come to find you.'

'I did my best to send you both a mind-message picture, but I realised that you are always chained up and that sometimes Chip cannot get out of the farmhouse.'

'Your mind-message was good. Chip said he saw you trapped in the old railway carriage in Bimblewick Wood. We tried to mind-message Farmer Parkin to search for you.... but she just kept telling us it was her over-active imagination. I wish Human Beans would sometimes take note of what we animals are saying.'

I collapsed in a heap inside Spud's kennel and he did his best to lick me warm. He cocked his head to one side as though inspecting me and said, 'I see the tips of your ears are still intact!' I nodded in response as he encouraged me to eat a little of his dog food. It was real meat scraps left over from Farmer Parkin's Sunday lunch and was delicious. Falling asleep inside his kennel and cuddling next to his furry body was bliss... and not an itchy flea in sight. They had all been annihilated by the frost.

CHAPTER 3

DRIVEN AWAY

'I'm warning you!' screeched the marmalade cat, Yarlminger. 'Keep away from our daytime snoozezone and NEVER come near us when we are hunting at night!' He snarled and whipped around, swishing his tail as though he would sweep me from the floor of the barn. I backed away, terrified of his claws and his vicious bite, only to bump into Clawit. Her strong, tawny front paw swiped at me in warning before she hissed, arched her back, puffed up her fur, and flattened her ears with fangs ready to strike.

'We'll pounce on you if you so much as steal a mouse tail,' growled Gobblechops, the fattest and greediest of the Wild Bunch, glaring at me from behind a tractor wheel with his great yellow eyes.

I crouched and mewed submissively and did not dare to move. I knew that the whole gang would not be able to resist chasing and bullying me if I so much as twitched a whisker.

'Go on then! Go and hide behind Spud as usual, you scaredy cat,' whined Glumteaser, using his usual snide way of provoking trouble and beginning to circle me menacingly. The scent of danger was all around as the mother sheep skittered in fear towards the barn walls, baaaing a warning to their bleating lambs to huddle close.

None of the Wild Bunch was courageous enough to fight me alone. But when they were together in a gang they felt strong and invincible. Their team hunting was to be admired, but their gang mentality was terrifying.

Suddenly a mottled brown body came hurtling down from the top of the hayloft. I could escape nowhere as Bumfleas landed on my back and rolled me over and over, digging his claws into my body and his fangs into my neck. The whole gang closed in to help injure me. My friend Spud was barking furiously out in the yard.

The next thing I knew Farmer Parkin was tackling the mobsters with her yard broom. 'Scat you idiots!' she yelled, as the spikes of her broom came crashing down on them. 'You are frightening my sheep and you will seriously injure that visitor and for what?'

I didn't wait to find out. My neck was bleeding and my body scarred on my back and stomach where Bumfleas had tugged out chunks of fur. I ran away as fast as my aching paws could take me. I could hear Spud calling me, but I was too frightened to stick around.

I headed across the lane and over the drystone wall to skirt the fields and get as far away as I could from the Wild Bunch. I never wanted to brave their cruelty again. Was that my third life gone? The sun was glistening calmly on the stretch of water that was a far-off reservoir in the valley below. The sky was a brilliant blue on the newly washed green fields. The snow had melted and everywhere felt fresh. At last my heart stopped pounding in my ears. I breathed deeply and felt the panic begin to leave me.

I could still run.... could still move fast enough to get away from danger; but I had had to leave behind my friends Spud and Chip. Sadness pricked behind my eyes, but tears would not do. I needed to get further away so that Yarlminger and his mates would not be tempted to follow.

My ears were alert for any sound. Hidden from the lane by the drystone walling, I now crept low on my belly uphill towards Bimblewick House. If I remembered correctly, it had plenty of outbuildings where I might find a hidey-hole.

Inkstink told me to rub my bleeding neck on some moss growing on a stone. As I rubbed it carefully, I winced now and then as the wound smarted and opened a little. However, it soon stopped bleeding and I rolled in the grass to clean my sticky fur. The rooks circling the tall trees surrounding Bimblewick House seemed to be telling me to draw closer.

A small number of ducks and geese were pecking at the rough grass for slugs and such. As I neared the walled garden of the house I could hear their usual quarrelsome noise. I was walking so stealthily and secretly that they did not take fright, but continued their pecking competition for the best grubs.

Bimblewick House must have been very grand indeed at one time, with a lily pond, a laburnum walk, woodlands, spacious lawns and a cricket pavilion. Now it was a haven for wildlife, as the wood rotted on the buildings and the pond and fields became overgrown and untended. I wondered if the creatures there would welcome me, or drive me away.

As I crouched low under a tree, I was startled by a voice above me.

'Looking for a free meal are you? I'm on a similar mission.' Perched low on a pine tree branch, I could see a huge blue and green bird in the shape of a lozenge. His long tail feathers drooped down impressively over his branch and his black beady eyes looked at me with intense curiosity.

'I'm Liberace the peacock. I'm named after a flamboyant pianist. Whatever that means. Pleased to meet you. But don't think you will steal my cat food the lady of the house puts out for me every day. I shall defend it with my honour.'

I wasn't quite sure what his 'honour' was, but I was worried that it might be his intensely sharp beak. It twitched as he cocked his head from side to side and eyed me down and along. I noticed he had a beautiful crown atop his head that shivered threateningly as he studied me.

I decided to sit pretty paws together and wash a droplet off my nose whilst I paused for thought. Then in mind-picture talk I said submissively, 'I promise not to steal your food, Sir, as long as you put in a good word for me with the lady of the house. Perhaps she would be kind enough to feed me too?'

'We shall see,' he said haughtily. 'I have already breakfasted and she will not feed me again until evening draws in. There are plenty of rats for you to catch around here. If I were you I would follow the geese and ducks. They peck at the feed Lord and Lady Bimblewick put out each morning; but the rats are very bold and will feed from their bowls in broad daylight.'

'Thank you for that advice! That's good to know,' I said, as I turned away to follow a worn track towards a walled garden.

The walled garden was entered through an arched doorway where the old oak door creaked, hanging half off its hinge. The ducks had abandoned their circular metal feeding trough in the centre of the cobbled area and were nonchalantly pecking in the herb borders for small edible creatures. I crept behind a scented bush that smelled like Nan Knitwarm's underwear drawer.

She used to make herb lavender bags and put them amongst her clothes and linen to make everything smell pleasant and to keep moths away. The memory overwhelmed me with a great wave of sadness and I wondered what had happened to my favourite Human Bean.

I was immediately alert however, when I saw a flurry of grey furry animals of mixed size rush upon the remains of the duck feed. They gathered eagerly around it, their pointed noses dipping into the feed and their shoulders hunching in satisfaction. RATS! Their noses and long worm-like tails quivered with excitement. My stomach made a small rumble of anticipation as I prepared for a creep along, a rush and a pounce.

Bang! Pow! Ping! Ping! Ding!

At the loud, ear-splitting noise I jumped higher than I ever remember and came clumsily down in a patch of nettles. Lord Bimblewick did not hear my screech, however, as he walked lazily over to the bodies of several dead rats. They lay in a ring around the feeding dish, like so many ninepins felled at a bowling alley.

His gun smoked as he gazed in satisfaction at his fallen victims. 'Gotcha, yer varmints!' he whooped as his wife came rushing out from the back porch in her pink nylon negligée.

'Harold, what on earth is going on!' she exclaimed. I had seen such things as her hairnet before on Nan Knitwarm, but I had never seen a Human Bean in pink, fluffy, bunny slippers before and I wondered why someone would be mad enough wear animal ears on their feet? Maybe they were a new fangled way of detecting earth tremors from seismic activity? Lady Bimblewick was trying to calm a cream, longhaired creature she repeatedly called Angel, which was wriggling and struggling in her arms.

'I've done it at last, Doris!' proclaimed Lord Harold Bimblewick. 'Got several blighters in one go when my gun pellets shattered in all directions off the metal feeder!'

'Well that's as maybe, but you scared

Angel and me half silly. Just warn us next time you go out with your shotgun, please.' Lady Doris Bimblewick let go of the mewing Angel, who scampered nervously back inside to the safety of the house. From my brief glimpse I deduced it was a feline creature of the longhaired, needing-grooming-each-day variety. She sported brown points on creamy fur, blue eyes and the sort of face, which looked as though it had bumped into someone's cricket bat at the time the cricket pavilion was built. I noticed a silly, diamanté collar sparkling somewhat around her indignant neck as she fled. Was that really a cat?

The geese and ducks were nowhere to be seen. At the first big bang they had squawked their way out to the safety of the meadow, away from any gun devilment and leaving behind a flurry of feathers. My paws stung from the nettles, but I was determined not to be spotted and mistaken for a rat, so skirted the walled garden under cover of the herb bushes until I spotted some ramshackle stables with peculiar occupants.

The old stone buildings with rotting doors smelled as though some sort of animals had been housed there a long time ago, but now there were cars.... several of them in different states of rusty ruin and others wrapped mysteriously from view. I crept beneath a blue, rectangular-roofed specimen with running board steps up to its doors, headlamps like protruding eyes and a leaking oil sump underneath. I thought the smell of oil was horrendous, but I was hoping it would keep all other animals away. I needed time to catch my breath, rest and heal.

Perhaps I could stay here underneath it until suppertime and then, when I heard Liberace cry for his evening meal, I could waylay Lady Doris and weave around her bunny slippers until she could not resist feeding me? I knew that female Human Beans were usually flattered by this sort of behaviour. I noticed the rooks were making a good meal of the dead rats around the duck feeder and I knew these scavengers would not think of leaving a scrap for me. Not a hope of a free meal there!

Despite the oil smell making me feel quite sick, at last I managed a good doze curled up on some greasy carpet. It must have been late afternoon when I was disturbed by Lord Harold's coming out to the stables to visit his 'Beauties'.

'My, my! My dearest Silver Ghost,' he crooned to a very old fashioned car parked against an oak pillar. He began stroking its silver-grey bodywork with a duster and surprised me by kissing its headlamp. I did not know that Human Beans could become so attached to lifeless things. He polished and crooned, rubbed and sighed as he worked. 'My Beauties! My Darlings! Ah my Humber Hawk!' His eyes alighted on a more streamlined car hidden under a huge tarpaulin. As he lifted it up to reveal the bonnet, I gasped at the amount of glinting, silver metal wear.... bumpers, badges, headlamps, grills.... all polished as shiny as mirrors. This car was obviously his favourite and although his house and outbuildings had fallen into disrepair, this was something he cared about and lovingly cleaned. Maybe this was what Noddle Newton was eying through his eyenoculars. Maybe this was what Newton was intending to steal?

Lord Harold sighed, rubbing and talking to his motor cars as the afternoon wore on. But I stayed stock still on the carpet under the blue, rectangular car with its wheel missing, its leaking oil sump and its wonky angel figurine gracing its bonnet. I dared not move. Lord Harold's shotgun was handily leaning against the wall nearby.

'Harold! Dinner!' shouted Lady Doris as she left a dish of cat food out for Liberace. Drat it! My plan to waylay her was no use. I dare not risk revealing myself to Lord Harold. He tenderly covered up his Humber Hawk car and went in for his dinner. It was just as well for my stomach began an awful rumbling.

I witnessed Liberace gobbling up everything he could from the dish Lady Doris had deposited.

I knew that with his sharp beak he could not possibly clean up the dish very well, so I approached nervously and asked, 'Do you mind terribly if I lick your leave takings?'

'Mind terribly? What is that supposed to mean?'

'Don't know really, but it just sounds polite. Did you hear the blast and see the rat carnage?'

'Nearly killed me with shock, it did.

Nearly fell off my branch with fright. Lord Harold is a pretty good shot with his gun. I hope he never decides that I am on the menu for Christmas dinner.'

'I am sure that you are too regal and decorative to be got rid of,' I reassured him as he nodded permission for me to lick clean his dish.

'Watch! This is how I impress people.' Liberace stood in a patch of late afternoon sunlight, glared into the distance and proceeded to fan out his majestic tail. It was magical and had big eye patterns in each tail feather.

'No wonder Lady Doris wants to keep you around. You certainly add a bit of glamour to the place. How do you think I could impress her?' I asked.

'Well she will not be too keen on cleaning up your fleas, but she might feel sorry for you if you show her your protruding ribs and hurt neck. She's not keen on presents of birds, rabbits or rats. Angel tried that and got her nose tapped for it.'

I was wondering how I was going to

survive another night without food. I was definitely too weak to hunt by now, my limbs aching and my neck throbbing. Liberace assured me that slugs and snails are very nutritious, but they tasted too slimy for my liking and clung like snot to my nose when I tried to lick them. He encouraged me to try eating a hibernating frog; but, when I poked at it with my paw, it blinked and jumped away into the lily pond before I could get a good taste. He soon gave up trying to help me and, as the sun began sinking, he returned to spend the night in his roost on a low branch. 'Watch out for the vixen,' he advised as he began arranging himself up above me. 'She is desperate to feed well before she births her cubs and she will smell your injury and hunt you down.'

Using *inkstink* he transmitted a mind picture of a dog-like creature with a bushy tail and a short, sharp snout. I felt frightened. How was I supposed to survive all these dangers and feed myself when I felt so weak? As night closed in, I knew I needed to get somewhere high up out of reach of the vixen. I thought about going back to the stables and climbing up on the roof of Humber Hawk.

CHAPTER 4

TRACKED

'How long have you been suspended in mid air?'

My whiskers tickled at the sound of a cat laughing and my ears twitched as I stirred with a great heavy weariness. I recognised the very welcome, familiar sound of Chip's voice.

'I thought you were done for. I traced your scent to Middle Moor and smelled blood. I thought the vixen, the she-fox, had eaten you. Then I picked up a paw trace and tracked you down to here. Voilà! I've brought you a present.'

It was a small dead mouse that he had dropped on the floor of the old stable. I slid down from the covered roof of the car and even before I thanked my friend I ate almost the whole of it. 'Thanks Chip! Thought you were ill? Thought I would never see you again?' I licked my chops appreciatively.

'True friendship does not give up at the first problem. Farmer Parkin soon had me well again and it was such a fine day, I determined to find out what had happened to you.'

'Chip, I do not want any more close encounters of the furred, outlaw kind. I cannot face that Wild Bunch again. They will definitely kill me if I come back to the farm.'

'Best not to risk it then,' Chip said thoughtfully. 'I have some news.... Farmer Parkin is getting married. She tells me her husband-to-be is another farmer who lives in the Peak District.'

'It sounds a bit hilly,' I mumbled miserably, suddenly visualizing the spiked peaks of Nan Knitwarm's lemon meringue pie.

'Spud and I have to move to another

farm many miles away. We will both be really sad to leave you,' said Chip soberly.

My heart skipped a beat and I found a strange tightness in my throat. I had made my first real animal friends and now I was going to lose them altogether.

'You and Spud have been so kind to me. How can I ever repay your friendship?' I whispered hoarsely.

'Ahh, That is a good question. In my experience we can pay back kindness by giving kindness. You pay it forwards instead of back. You will find some Human Bean or some other creature to be kind to, I'm sure, and you will make new friends. You are a friendly chap after all. However, you are in no fit state to feed yourself. I will do a little more hunting for you before nightfall and then head back to the farm. It's tough to be saying goodbye.'

I nodded and felt so weak that I crawled inside an old, broken, woven log basket to rest, whilst I watched him pad out through the door of the building. He swished his tail in farewell and went off to do as he promised.

My late afternoon nap did not last long. I heard the sharp clatter of horse hooves on the cobbles in the huge yard. 'Whoa Ragnar! Calm down you silly beast!' yelled a woman's voice, reining in a huge, black horse.

I dodged back under the Humber car and saw the fluffy pink rabbit slippers come running out of the house followed by Angel's paws. 'What on earth is the matter, dear Mrs. Thwackit?' panted Lady Doris's breathless voice.

'Oh just to warn you that the drag hunt is coming through tomorrow. Lots of extra hounds up here along with their hunting team. Thought I had better give you the tip-off, then you can keep your animals in.'

'Very thoughtful of you my dear! I shall keep the geese in and of course my lovely Angel who is terrified of hounds. Liberace will keep up in the trees as usual if he scents the hunting dogs around.'

'Best to be on the safe side. By the way, are you any capstones missing from your stone walls? Someone has been daring to steal them from the bottom meadow perimeter. They daren't do that so near the house or Thunder would set up a racket.'

'No, nothing missing at the moment. That Thunder of yours is a really good guard dog! We haven't noticed anything out of the ordinary lately, apart from Angel being a bit spooked by something.'

'Angel maybe smells the vixen about. That wily fox has been taking new lambs from Merryweather's farm down in the valley. Pity we are not allowed to hunt it down.'

'Well the drag hunt may well turn into a real hunt if the hounds get its scent and that would be the end of her and her cubs.'

I made a mental note of a need to make myself invisible the following day when the hounds would be scenting around. I did not like the sound of the words 'hunt it down.' It felt scary, like the bullying I had received at the claws of the Wild Bunch.

Then Mrs. Thwackit slapped her horse on its ample rump with her whip and Ragnar obediently wheeled around and clopped out of the yard, carrying his mistress away along the lane towards his stabling.

Could this now be my opportunity to charm Lady Doris Bimblewick? Nothing ventured. Nothing gained. I crept out from underneath the Humber car and lay full length across the cobbled path into the house, so that neither she nor Angel could possibly ignore me.

Angel reacted before Lady Doris had a bunny hop's chance to do so and arched her back, staring at me in an alarmed way. But the ears of the pink rabbit slippers waggled at me and almost tripped over me before I heard, 'Oh what a poor, poor creature! Starved and injured and in need of some TLC. We shall have to share some of your gourmet food my dear Angel.... Agh! But do not go anywhere near that flea-bitten creature. You will catch something nasty. We will keep it in the cricket pavilion!'

With a swoop Lady Doris clutched up her darling Angel and disappeared into the house. A few minutes later she emerged, slamming the back door very firmly behind her, but clutching a tempting bowl of strange smelling cat food. I followed her rabbit slippers, flip-flopping down the path to the mouldering cricket pavilion. So.... she seemed sorry for me and was going to give me somewhere comfortable to stay and more importantly something to eat!

What followed afterwards was in no way comforting. After I had gobbled some of the gourmet food.... not really understanding what creature a gourmet might be.... the fussing lady reappeared with a comb, some nasty smelling liquid in a bowl and lots of cotton wool. I was crooned to whilst she combed me. Then she tutted in disgust. She pulled at snags in my coat and dabbed at me with the liquid that made my cuts smart. I almost scratched her, but thought better of it. Better to put up with all her TLC, whatever that was, and still get food than have her throw me out into the lane.

Her TLC did not last too long, thank goodness, before she disappeared in a flurry of fluffy slippers and firmly closed the door of the cricket pavilion. It began to grow dark, but the moon was up and shining in at me through the grimy spider-webbed windows. I wasn't too sure what a cricket pavilion was designed for exactly, but it had wooden benches and double doors leading out onto a field. It had the sort of overhanging roof with support posts you see on a fancy verandah. But this wasn't anything fancy. Its paint was peeling and its floorboards were rotting. There was a very strange animal smell I did not recognise.

Lady Doris had seemed very kind. She had fed me, groomed me and tended to my wounds, but she had forgotten the most important thing.... I had no water.

Perhaps she was going to get me some in the morning. My throat was so dry. I jumped up on one of the benches and licked the condensation from the inside of a window.

I could see the moon was up over the fields by now and it bathed everywhere in silver light. It was a beautiful, frosty evening and everything in my *inkstink* told me I should be outside. I thought I glimpsed a small, dog-like creature creep out from under the wooden pavilion and scent its way around the field. That must be the vixen searching for food. No wonder there was a funny smell inside the pavilion. She had her den right under those rotten floorboards. I needed to get right away from there.

By morning when the hounds of the drag hunt arrived they would maybe scent her and surround the pavilion. I panicked and tried to find an escape route. I tried scratching at a rotten floorboard, but apart from crumbling a bit on the surface it still stood strong. I tried jumping at the door handle, but I just kept falling backwards and was becoming very weak again. Then I felt worn out after my scary day, so I decided to curl up on an old, woollen coat, flung across one of the benches and pretend I was back in Nan Knitwarm's snug house keeping her feet warm. At least no one would disturb me here.... or so I thought.

I dozed fitfully and began dreaming of a lovely fireside and Nan Knitwarm's cosy lap. I imagined her knitting one of her voluminous, woollen sweaters. She always looked extra cuddly when she finally wore what she knitted. Oh the memory....!

I was suddenly startled awake by a scratching at the pavilion door. 'Tigger are you there?' mewed a familiar voice. 'I sent you a mind-picture to signal me where you were; but you ignored me. I scented your paw trail. I have brought you my night's catch.'

'Chip, you're such a good friend. I really need to get out of this building. The vixen has her den under here and tomorrow there is going to be a drag hunt. When the hounds smell her, they will surround the cricket pavilion. They might even mistake me for a young fox cub!'

'Hang on in there, Tigger. I have to consider how I might rescue you.'

I did not have the strength to hang anywhere. I just sat on the coat and waited.... and waited.... and waited.

Chip seemed to be considering for a very long time. There was a tantalising smell of his night's catch drifting under the door.

'There's a rain barrel with a lid by the door, so I will jump up on it and take a closer look at how I might press open the latch.' There was a thud as he landed on the lid of the barrel and something that sounded like metal clattering, as he made several attempts to press down the thumb latch of the door.

'I have tried with my forepaw, but that is evidently not strong enough,' he grunted. 'I will try again using my hind leg.' There was a good deal of scrabbling and exasperated meowing before I heard the latch click down and lift. I had never really mastered the art of curling my paw around a door to pull it open, but I suddenly felt inspired to try. When I heard the latch lift for the second time, I pulled at the door and it inched open.

Chip and I rubbed along each other in greeting and then we decided to pick up his night's catch and run away with it before the vixen came back. We silently edged along the grass verge of the lane opposite Bimblewick House and escaped to the warmth of the deep wood. I shivered, however, as we crept past the old railway carriage which had cost me my second life.

'There's an abandoned badger set on the edge of the wood,' said Chip comfortingly. 'You could snuggle in there for the night to stay warm. However, in the morning you will need to be smart and get up somewhere high away from the hounds. The hunting people will bring a small terrier dog with them. They like using it to sniff out things in burrows and holes, so be warned!'

'It sounds like a Jack Russell dog to me. We had a kind neighbour called Mrs. Benchsit who lived opposite Nan Knitwarm's house, but she had a terrifying Jack Russell who always threatened to rip me apart.'

'That's the type! Best avoided altogether if you ask me,' warned Chip. 'So I wonder where you will find a forever home, young chap? Have you thought about venturing further along the lane and testing out the cottage where the children live?'

The thought of the laughing children brought back painful memories of being teased and having stones thrown at me in Nan Knitwarm's street. 'No! I couldn't possibly bear to be near children. They are always so cruel!'

'I think you will find that is quite untrue,' Chip advised me. 'I once used to think that ALL people who wore Wellington boots were cruel, after being kicked about by an angry man wearing them; but it was not true. Farmer Parkin was so generous to me. She took me in from the cold and looked after me; but she always wears wellies to work in the farmyard. Mind you, it took me a while to conquer my fear of them. I used to make a big, suspicious circle around her pair, whenever they stood in the back porch all by themselves. Once I understood that it was whoever was wearing the Wellingtons that was the important thing, I was OK. I think it is what Human Beans call being prejudiced.... Prejudging something or someone just because you have had one nasty experience.'

'Have you met the children from the cottage, Chip?'

'Not exactly met, but they stop to say kind words to me on their way home from school and I have seen and heard them playing with their kittens and petting Mrs. Thwackit's dog and horses. They seem to respect animals. They laugh when they are happy, not because they want to taunt and tease and be cruel.'

'Perhaps I am prejudiced against children,' I admitted. I thought for a moment that it might be something I needed to change about myself.

The old, abandoned badger set smelled very odd, but was clean and warm inside, deep underground. We finished eating our evening meal companionably, then groomed and washed each other. Afterwards Chip said in a peculiar, wobbly voice, 'I need to leave you now, Tigger.

It has been good to know you and advise a young chap such as yourself. Farmer Parkin has packed all our belongings into big boxes and, as the sun rises, there will be a leave-taking of the farm in a huge van called a pantechnicon.'

I was unable to reply. My throat seemed to have ceased up with something gluey. I tried to prrp my thanks to him, but it just came out like a funny squeak. *Inkstink* told me he knew how grateful I was for all his help and that our friendship was something he would always treasure. He crawled away out of the badger set and into the moonlight. He wanted to make sure he was back in the farmhouse before deep cold set into the night. 'Pan...tech....ni... con' The word had a strange lonely feel about it, like something tugging at my heart strings.

I slept fitfully, my whiskers, ears and nose alert for any signs of danger. I could not bear the thought of being cornered underground by a terrier dog. At first light I crept out from my hiding place and peered around. My long-range vision was best when something was moving.

I could see a couple of magpies perched on the apex of a tall, stone barn along the lane next to Bimblewick House. They took off into the air at intervals, looking for morning tit-bits amongst the roof moss in the gutters. That was a really high place. Then I noticed that some Human Bean had made an attempt to stop the barn collapsing by strengthening the crumbling walls with wooden beam-braces. They started at ground level and leaned up the building almost to the roof. Would I be able to climb them? I needed to find out quickly.

So that I would not be noticed, I crept low to the ground as my mother had taught me and skipped across the lane before considering my climb up to the barn roof. However, the silly birds had already started alarm calls; so I needed to get up there quickly before I could be bagged or attacked. Nan Knitwarm had usually clipped my claws quite short, but since my weeks on the moors they had grown long and very, very sharp. I found that, if I dug my claws into the rough wood of the brace, I could clutch my way along and up.

My fear of falling was very strong, but even stronger was the fear that something might get me from the ground.... a Human Bean, a dog, or a fox. I edged up a few inches at a time, not daring to look down. I was fortunate that it was a brightening morning with little wind. At last I just had to make my last leap over the gutter onto the roof. I summoned what little strength I had left and pushed with all my might with my hind legs.

Suddenly I missed my footing and clung for dear life to the edge of the gutter. For a moment I thought I would fall metres to my death below. Somehow I was given a rush of courage and was able to scrabble my way up to safety. Had I just spent my fifth life? Maybe! I had been dumped on the moors, trapped in a railway carriage, ganged up on by the Wild Bunch, locked in a cricket pavilion and now I had nearly fallen to my death. Whatever next? It really was time to find my forever home before all my nine lives ran out.

The morning sun began to rise and warm my fur as I sat on the barn roof-ridge. The breeze tickled my whiskers and sent my nose tantalising aromas of rodents - rats, mice, voles, and shrews. It was no use wishing I could hunt for food up here. I would have to banish any thought of breakfast until the danger of the hounds was past.

It was amazing that, from this vantage point, I could see far down the lane to the farm where Spud nosed out of his kennel to warm himself as the sun rose. Soon all the belongings from the farm would be packed away in the pantechnicon and he and Chip would be whizzed away from me forever.

As I clung grimly to the roof ridge, the warmth of the sunshine and the chattering of the early birds could not ease the deep sadness in my heart that morning.

I espied Farmer Parkin feeding Spud and busying herself with herding a few sheep and their young lambs out from the barn into the farm trailer. Spud helped round them up in his usual efficient way, cornering the ones who were hesitating and guiding them up the ramp. He soon had them all inside. They bleated anxiously and nosed the fresh air through the side slats of the truck. I felt sorry for them. I remembered that feeling of being trapped and shut in. It was not pleasant.

Soon there was a loud, roaring noise as the biggest removal van I had ever seen swayed around the corner by Bimblewick Wood and accelerated its way along the lane towards the farm. Was that the pantechnicon? As its brakes squealed by the farm gate, a swarm of Human Beans in t-shirts and black sweatpants jumped out and began to buzz around the farmhouse. Farmer Parkin began giving them detailed instructions. The strangest objects were finding their way into the giant van; a chair with rocking legs which seemed to move of its own accord; a tall wooden hall clock with a cuckoo bird coming out singing 'uckoo' in a weird, strangled voice; a stool with only three legs, a kitchen table with four scratching posts supporting it. The men worked ceaselessly, more like scurrying ants than busy bees.

I watched fascinated as the pantechnicon swallowed all the contents being carried out of the farmhouse by the busy removal men. They loaded everything up its tailgate and into its gaping mouth. It seemed magical that a van could hold so many pieces of furniture and boxes. I wondered if it had indigestion. I lost count of how many items it had gobbled before I became dangerously dizzy.

Then I saw Spud's chain being unlocked from its ring and his kennel being lifted onto the removal van. It was the last item to be loaded before the men closed its huge doors. Spud nosed around the farmyard relishing his short spell of freedom. Then he was scooped into the front seat of Farmer Parkin's four-wheel drive to accompany her on the way to their new farmhouse. But where was Chip? For a moment I selfishly hoped he would be left behind; but no.

Farmer Parkin left the engine running and got out of her Landrover. She checked that the trailer carrying the sheep was hooked on safely. She then went into the farmhouse for the last time. She emerged with a shoulder bag, an electric kettle and a wicker cat-carrier with something black and white inside. I could hear a faint mew as Chip objected to the movement of his basket. Farmer Parkin had not left him behind after all. She looked around the farmyard wistfully one last time. Perhaps she had been happy there and had fond memories. She locked the door with her house key, posted it through the letterbox by the gate and got into her vehicle. She accelerated away, towing the sheep truck and slowly following the swaying pantechnicon.

As it negotiated the bend in the narrow lane I could just see the tip of a wet, doggy nose sticking out from the partially open, passenger window. 'Goodbye farm! Goodbye moors! Goodbye my friend Tigger!' I heard Spud say.

'Goodbye Tigger Digger,' mewed a smaller sad voice, as the vehicles drove into the distance and disappeared.

CHAPTER 5

HOUNDED

I tried so hard not to cry, but my eyes could not help watering. I had found such wonderful friends and here they were disappearing from my life just like Nan Knitwarm. Was that part of life.... losing people you loved and grew attached to? It certainly seemed so. Now I would have to find new friends. But, 'Watch out!' I told myself, 'You will slip and fall down the barn roof if you do not take care!'

I was soon shaken from my 'feeling sorry for myself' mood as the morning stirred. A car, with two grown-ups in the front seats and two children in the back, whizzed by from the cottage up the lane.

I guessed it was a family on their way to work and school. Then I heard Mrs. Thwackit soothing one of her horses by her stables and the snort and clomp of that big, black horse, Ragnar. It really was my breakfast time, but no food for me this morning. My stomach would just have to rumble. The hounds of the drag hunt were due.

The first sign that something was happening was the thrum of vehicles groaning up the nearby hills and coming from several directions to the little crossroads by the farm. Slowly they turned into Bimblewick Lane and parked one behind the other just below the barn on which I was crouching. I could hear whining and excited yowling coming from the vehicles. The hounds had arrived! I thought I had better crouch below the roof ridge in case they noticed me. Several men and one or two women in green jackets emerged from an assortment of landrovers and jeeps.

Some of them let hounds out of the back of their vehicles.

One man, wearing a flat cap and a puffed up jacket, held a can of something stinky in his hand. I could smell the horrible smell as the breeze wafted from the north. The man kept down wind of the hounds and skirted the drystone walls to reach a field in the distance. I could see his dipping a rag into the smelly can and then setting off to trail it behind him.... over field and wall, through Bimblewick Wood, over the farthest meadow, then down to the valley below.

The hounds were on leashes but seemed eager to nose each other and wag their tails in greeting. They were sniffing each other with great relish. It reminded me of how hungry I felt.

They rubbed and wagged and huddled together around some sort of leader.... a tall, thin, long-legged Human Bean in a fitted green jacket, black helmet, riding boots and cream, leg-hugging riding trousers.

'Smart jodhpurs Thomas! Here is your

hunting horn!' shouted Mrs. Thwackit above the noise of the hounds. She sat astride Black Ragnar, similarly dressed to Thomas in what I assumed to be her hunting gear. She handed him a shiny instrument of some sort. The jod-purr trousers did not seem impressed and did not seem to be purring to me. Suddenly, there was such a din with the dogs getting excited and even more so when Thomas tried out his hunting horn. 'Doo doo! Doo doo!' went his awkward attempt at blowing it, as the assortment of hounds yapped, and barked even louder.

The hunting riders must have decided to wear some sort of school uniform, for they all appeared in similar dark, green jackets, black riding helmets and cream jodhpurs (the non purring variety) as they led their troupe of snorting horses out of their trailers.

Then I spotted a terrier! This low-slung variety of dog was released from the front seat of a jeep by a Human Bean, wearing a flat cap and what looked like a waxed raincoat. A shotgun similar to Lord Bimblewick's hung down from his arm.

'Heel, Snapper!' he yelled, his face a crimson snarl similar to that of his dog. The terrier was straining on the leash as though he would like to head towards the Bimblewicks' cricket pavilion. His snout snuffled along the verge, breathing in a trace of something *very interesting*. Maybe it was my scent or maybe it was that of the vixen? Thank goodness his master had other plans and was insistent he kept to heel for now. He yanked him roughly in.

The whole group of strange Human Beans seemed to have some sort of time signal inside their heads which said, 'Bring out the flasks and hot drinks.' For the next little while they stood or sat about chatting and drinking something from their steaming mugs. They swayed about on their horses, or sat on the tailboards of their trailers.

Then without warning the tall, gangly man broke away from his brood of foxhound fans and began to hurdle over

the low stone walls like an Olympic medalist.... or maybe more like a jumping flea! I had never seen such enthusiasm for jumping in a Human Bean before.
At a sudden loud blast from Thomas's wonky horn, the hounds were released and broke into two streams of dogs. They scoured the field before them, following the stinky scent that they craved. I was startled but very impressed by their teamwork.

A great cheer went up from the Human Beans. The people following the hounds made sure they kept together as a pack. They waved their sticks in the air and followed their lead. They soon found their way over a wooden stile into the next field in hot pursuit.

I held my breath, as a few moments later the riders kicked their horses into action and trotted from the lane through the first farm gate into the field. They were off, streaming across the field and ready for their gallop up to their first jump of the day. There was a great deal of thwacking and hurrahing, a great deal of charging at the drystone wall. Most of the horses cleared it, but not quite as effortlessly as Thomas, the man with the long, gangly legs.

One poor horse, I think it was Black Ragnar, clipped his hoof on the wall. As he jumped he threw off his rider. I understood now why all the riders were wearing protective helmets.

No one seemed concerned. The rider must have been unhurt, because I could just glimpse her climbing back onto the black horse. The horse whinnied and limped along, obviously in some sort of pain, but his rider urged him on across the next field and the next.... into the distance, following the hunt.

'Interesting behaviour!' commented one of the magpies that had decided to risk landing and perched precariously near me on the roof. I was leaning against the ridge and clinging for dear life onto the mossy roof tile below it.

'I just do not want to risk being

hounded,' I replied, as a gust of wind flurried the fur around my head making me wobble. 'I think I have already spent five of my nine lives!'

'That lot would make short work of you if they caught you,' said the magpie not succeeding in trying to cheer me up. 'Human beings hunt for sport, you know.... not out of hunger. That horse will have to be treated by a vet at great cost. Some injury happens to some poor animal every time there is a hunt!'

'It seems there are lots of different types of Human Bean,' I replied thoughtfully. 'Some are kind and considerate and some seek only their own pleasure. I suspect most of them are sort of in between the two. I'm looking for a forever home with someone kind. They don't have to be perfect.'

'You need to try at the cottage up the lane. The Smiths already have two kittens, but the whole family seems quite nice to me. If their kittens bring them presents of dead mice or voles they put them out in the lane for us to eat. It is very handy for us.... and very considerate of them with food constantly at our beak and call.'

With that he cawed and took to the air to find his mate, leaving me wondering how much longer I would be able to cling on.

Time seemed to pass so slowly. I could see through the kitchen window of Bimblewick house that Lady Doris was feeding Angel by the sink. She crooned to her and stroked her, as the longhaired creature delicately dipped her nose into her gourmet cat food. Perhaps Lady Doris's bunny slippers would come searching for me at the cricket pavilion and she would wonder what had happened to me? There seemed no sign of the vixen. Maybe she had got wind of the hunt and decided to disappear for a while in the opposite direction.

Lord Bimblewick came out to the ducks and geese in their pen and scattered their morning grain. However, today he did not let them out into the meadow. He took a bird feeder up to Liberace's tree and stretched tall to hang it up, so that the peacock would not have to come down to feed this morning. I could just glimpse Liberace winking appreciatively. Then Lord Bimblewick headed for his Humber Hawk and began to tenderly polish his vintage car. I wished upon a beam of sunlight that I would be able to find people who would treat me so kindly. I knew it was pointless trying to be accepted at Bimblewick House. Angel was not a tolerant cat.

Lady Doris did eventually emerge from her kitchen with another dish of food intended for me, but when she saw that the cricket pavilion door was creaking on its hinge and that I was nowhere in sight, she shook her head, shrugged her shoulders and went back inside to give Angel a second helping. My stomach gave a noisy groan of disappointment.

Towards noon, when the sun was at its

highest, I heard the sound of the hunting horn. The hunt was returning and the horses clopping along the lane up from the crossroads near the farmhouse. Thomas, the gangly-legged man, led the way, breathing hard now, as the hounds yapped excitedly at his heels. Then their owners put them on leashes and enticed them back to their trailers with some sort of meaty reward to eat. My stomach let out another rumble as I crouched once more, ducking my head down below the roof ridge. I knew that I would not be able to breathe properly again until every hound and that terrier dog, Snapper, was back in its vehicle. Nearly all in! Last dog locked up! Ahh! I relaxed my grip a little and nearly slipped off the roof.

However, I was proved right. It was Black Ragnar who had been injured. By now he was limping dramatically. Mrs. Thwackit looked thunderous as she followed behind Thomas, leading her horse instead of riding him.

'No, I won't be able to join you at the Hare and Hounds for lunch, Thomas. I will have to stay until the vet arrives to treat this stupid horse,' she complained as she led Ragnar by his reins back into his stabling. Thomas tossed her the hunting horn and got into the passenger seat of someone else's four-wheel drive.

I decided there and then that it was no use begging a home from the Thwackits. Impatience with animals seemed the order of the day. I felt so sorry for Ragnar. He had misjudged a jump and should have been treated for his injured leg immediately, but Mrs. Thwackit had been so intent on continuing with the hunt that she had not bothered about him until now. He was obviously in a great deal of pain. I knew about vets. Visits to or from them usually entailed needles and pills. I did not envy Ragnar one little bit.

The rest of the hunt dispersed and went for a pub lunch down in the village.

I was still teetering on the barn roof and wondering about risking coming down, when I spied two children being dropped off by a school bus at the crossroads. The bus roared away leaving them to walk up the lane. The girl seemed a little taller than her brother and was feeling a little sad as she complained, 'We're going to miss talking to Chip and Spud on our way home from school. I wonder how they will like their new farm?'

'They'll probably feel a little bit strange, just like we did when we first moved up here and didn't know anyone. They're really friendly animals. They'll soon feel happier and settle in. It will be a bigger, more exciting farm for them,' said the boy, as he kicked a stone along the lane below me. I decided to step over my fear of children and risk a mew to see what would happen.

'Did you hear that, Drew?' said the girl.

'What?' her brother replied, stopping and listening.

'Mew!' I cried, reminding myself more of a timid lamb than a cat.

‘I can hear a cat crying. Is it Sofa or Cassandra? They might be stuck somewhere,’ insisted the girl.

I decided it was time to reveal myself and stood right up on top of the roof ridge, my pointy ears and raised tail back-lit by the afternoon sun.

‘Look up there. It’s a striped cat,’ said Drew pointing skywards.

‘I wonder how he will get down. It seems a big, scary drop,’ said the girl.

‘Clara, there’s some stone steps by the side of the barn up to the hayloft door. Maybe we can reach him up there?’

They both ran around into the Bimblewicks’ yard and climbed up the stone steps built against the side of the barn.

‘I can’t reach him from here,’ Clara complained, standing on the very top of the flight of stone steps and stretching her arms up towards the roof ridge. ‘Maybe Dad will be able to do it when he comes home from work. He’s tall and has very long arms.’

‘I’ll tell Lord Harold and maybe he will

fetch a ladder,' suggested Drew.

I had no intention of being caught again by the Bimblewicks and put back into the cricket pavilion, so when Lord Harold did arrive with a set of ladders and tried to entice me towards the edge of the gutter, I stubbornly stayed on the roof ridge.

After a lot of huffing and puffing up and down the ladder Clara and Drew finally brought their parents to view the situation. They each tried to entice me to the edge of the roof with a dish of food.

The sun was beginning to set by now and the wind was getting cold. Lord Harold and Lady Doris advised everyone to leave the cat food on top of the stone steps and go indoors.

'When he is hungry and cold enough he will find his own way down. After all, he found his own way up,' reassured Mrs. Smith, the children's mother, as she led them away. 'Let's go in for dinner. We will all catch our death out here!'

I wasn't too sure what catching a death would be like, but it did not sound very pleasant. I would rather catch a mouse!

I waited until everyone had disappeared indoors and then I tried my best to get down. It seemed sensible to try and jump onto the wooden support beam where I had first crawled up. However, I did not have the courage to jump onto it from the gutter. It seemed to stretch dangerously down and down and made me dizzy just to look at it.

I tentatively moved towards the side of the building, where the stone steps came up from the yard to the hayloft door. I could smell the dish of tantalising cat food and urged myself to jump down, but in my mind's eye I kept seeing a vision of Ragnar's hurt leg as it had banged against stone. It put me off jumping.

I prayed to the Light of Heaven to help me. I had run out of courage and ideas. At the back of the building Lord Harold had left his ladder leaning up against the gutter. He had strapped it close to the wall so that it would not blow down in the wind. I sat at the gutter edge and realised that there was no way I would be able to climb down headfirst. I would break my neck.

The two magpies I had seen earlier settled for a moment on the roof ridge. I expected them to laugh at my predicament, but the male cawed, 'You will have to go down backwards and fall from one rung to the next.' They seemed to be birds full of curiosity so they decided to stick around to see what I would do next.

It was the only way. 'The Light of Heaven protect me! Please!' I prayed. I concentrated all my thoughts on balancing well, as I clung with my front paws to the gutter and eased my body over the edge so that I was dangling. 'Here goes with my leap of faith,' I thought, as I let go and aimed to catch the first rung of the ladder a metre or so below.

I breathed in a glorious breath of light
and allowed myself to fall, clutching
out for the highest rung. Suddenly
my forelegs ached with the strain as
I succeeded.... the weight of my body
dependent on the strength of my two
shoulders, strong paws and ten claws. I
only paused for the briefest of breaths

and then repeated my little falls several times. I fell from rung to rung until I could sense the ground safely near. At last I landed firmly on the stone cobbles of the yard.

'Well done!' cawed the magpie that had helped me, as he and his female mate took flight to find their roost in the wood for the night. 'Remember this is your sixth life lost. Time to find your forever home!'

CHAPTER 6

GROUNDED

I wasted no time in dallying near Bimblewick House. I quickly gobbled the meal put out for me at the top of the hayloft steps. Then I sent a thought of farewell to Liberace. I skirted the Thwackit Stables as Thunder, their guard dog, came out to bark at me. The wind took up its howling shriek over the moors, as he chased me along the lane from his territory. My heart was pounding. However, he must have decided that chasing me was not worth the effort. He gave up and soon returned to his kennel to get warm.

But where could I go to get warm?

I knew that Clara and Drew would be settling into their own beds for the night and would be unlikely to search for me, or take me inside their cottage. I thought of returning to the badger set in Bimblewick Wood, but decided I would rather risk exploring nearer to the Smith family home.

The howling wind had chased the clouds from the sky and now the moon was up, shrouding everything in silver light. I soundlessly padded along the lane until I reached the pretty house with what I recognised as wisteria growing around the front porch. I remembered something Nan Knitwarm had once said to me. 'Hysteria, wisteria! There's no denying you wind around my heart like that twining plant, Mr. Tigger Digger!' She had rubbed me and tickled me, her eyes dancing with love and a broad beam on her face. I missed her. Where was she now, I wondered?

The eyes of the cottage were closed, but a faint glow of light came through the curtains. It all looked so cosy. I sent a wish on a moonbeam that I would one day be allowed inside. I crept along the garden path and around to the back. Yes, there were more buildings behind the stone cottage. I would search for shelter there.

I paused and listened. There was a crunching sound as though a creature was munching something. I sniffed an animal trail along the gravel path. It smelled like something I recognised.... a hedgehog. I knew better than to disturb him as he crunched the snails he had found at the base of the garden wall. I remembered getting my nose prickled as a small kitten and didn't fancy repeating the experience. He carried on munching, ignoring me and knowing he could curl up in a protective ball if I as much as drew close.

'I'm not looking to harm you,' I said wistfully, 'I just need to find somewhere warm for the night. Any suggestions?'

'I've just come out of hibernation from a log pile, but I am not keen to share it with anyone, especially not a cat,' he snuffled. 'You could try the workshop. The owner sometimes forgets to close the door properly and I often go in there to find creepy crawlies for my supper.' He did not spare me a further glance, but carried on hunting for delicious snails.... Well delicious to him. 'Slimy as snot, more like!' I thought.

By the light of silver moonbeams I could make out the wooden, painted entrance to the workshop. The door was a little ajar and held in place against the wind by a large effigy of a dragon. I knew it wasn't real as it smelled more of metal than anything alive, but it did have alarmingly beady eyes, a large-fanged snarl and a huge, scaly body. I pretended to snarl back at it, just to give myself a little more courage and strode past him swishing my tail, just in case he was magic and decided to become real.

The stone building was very old, but the roof trusses looked new and the roof recently rebuilt with a skylight flooding the area with moonlight. There were wonderful and fascinating smells....

garden tools with earthy smells, rags with oily smells, hanging baskets with dried, forlorn old herbs, and YES, a bale of hay tucked under the workbench. I scrabbled up onto it, ducking my head beneath the workbench just in time. Then I set about kneading the hay into a luxurious nest where I might snuggle.

I did not take me long to fall asleep and I remembered Chip's advice to curl my tail around my head, nose and ears, just in case it got frosty. 'What a day,' I sighed as I drifted off into dreamland.

I woke at first light with the sound of blackbirds shrilling in the trees around the garden. I needed to get up early and try to get the family to notice me before they went to work and school. I decided to place myself outside their back door, because it smelled as though that was their greatest foot-traffic area. I could hear the sounds of their morning breakfast in the kitchen - muffled chatting, plates and dishes scraping. I was hungry again!

I suspected they would soon be

coming out of the house, so I positioned myself right outside the back door and lay down on my side, so that they could see my protruding ribcage and feel sorry for me. I sensed it was time for them to leave, but they did not emerge this morning and the yard cobbles were very cold. Hurry up and notice me! I sent all four of them a mind picture to see if it would get any response.

I did not have to wait long. Clara emerged with a handful of crumbs for the birds and almost tripped over me. I was tempted to run away, but I plucked up courage and stayed still where I was for the best dramatic effect.

'Ma! Pa!' she cried. 'Our prayers were answered. The striped cat got down and here he is outside waiting for his breakfast!'

The family gathered around me very gently, not wishing to scare me away.

'What a poor, thin creature,' said Ma. 'He must have been dumped on the moors and been living wild.'

'Look how thin he is,' sympathised Pa.

'His ribs are sticking out and he has a wound on his neck.'

Clara risked stroking me very gently. 'His fur is very stiff and scratchy like a doormat. I bet he has worms and fleas.'

'Better not let him near Cassie and Sofa, then. They might catch something nasty. What shall we do with him Ma?' asked Drew.

'I'll feed him out here for now and keep the kittens indoors. We'll try grooming him when he's less hungry and I'll treat him for fleas and worms.'

'Good job it's Saturday and we don't have to go anywhere in particular today,' said Pa. 'We can phone the Cat Sanctuary in the valley and see if they have room for him. Sofa and Cassandra aren't going to like having an adult, male cat around!'

Clara continued to stroke me gently whilst Ma went inside to get me food and medicine. Pa went inside to use the telephone.

'I wish we could keep him, Clara. Sofa sleeps on your bed and Cassie with Ma and Pa. I would really appreciate a cat of my own,' said Drew.

'That would be lovely for you Drew. But we do have to think about Sofa and Cassie. They might be frightened of him.'

I don't think so,' Drew corrected. 'Remember when we first let the kittens out in the garden and Thunder came round to inspect them? They spat at him and tried to claw his nose. They chased him away before they finally made friends with him.'

I couldn't imagine making friends with the Thwackits' retired foxhound, but I could imagine sleeping on a real bed snuggled up to the boy. I thought this pair of youngsters really seemed to want to help me. Maybe I was gradually learning to overcome my prejudice against children?

Ma came out of the house with a dish of delicious food and enticed me to eat, whilst she gently untangled my fur with a special comb. It tugged my skin, but I was too hungry to respond to the pain of it and carried on gobbling.

'Slow down young chap or you will be sick,' Ma advised. But I couldn't. There was something in my brain which told me to eat as quickly and as much as possible. Perhaps being half starved does that to you?

Then I smelled the flea and worming medicine that I knew would be put on the skin at the back of my neck. It would feel cold and trickle, making me shiver. I didn't wait around for that. I tried to run away, but Drew threw a coat over me so that I could not see where I was going and Clara enveloped me in it, whilst Ma got me with the stinky stuff on my neck. Yuck!

'There!' cried Ma. "You are all fed and treated my boy.'

I wondered what to do next. I was ready for a nap by a fire if there was one going, but then Pa came out of the cottage shaking his head. 'I'm afraid Celia's rescue shelter is full. She can't take any more cats at the moment. She suggests we keep him here and feed him outside until she's homed a cat and there's room for him.'

'Can't we have a third cat?' asked Drew hopefully.

'I think we have enough mouths to feed already,' said Pa, 'and the kittens will not like it if their home feels invaded.'

'Come on you two. Leave him to his own devices. He probably needs to find his way about the garden. We'll call him for food twice a day with the porch bell.'

With that they all went inside and I could hear Clara and Drew calling Sofa and Cassandra to play with them. If only I could be one of those kittens.

The next few days were filled with warm spring sunshine and I began to settle into some sort of a routine. I would stir from my hay nest in the workshop and go hunting in the fields at first light, or as night fell. With barns, hedgerows and woods to explore it was quite exciting. Then I would find a nice patch of soil in the cottage garden to use as a toilet; or if the ground was too hard I could usually find a molehill on a verge. I would dig a deep hole and meticulously bury anything I deposited in it. Then, when I heard the first sounds of human activity, I would crouch behind a shrub in the cottage garden, waiting for the porch bell to ring, which hung outside the kitchen door.

It seemed to be the children's task to feed me. They enjoyed taking turns to ring the brass bell very vigorously. This was to alert me to come quickly when the fresh food was first put out. It was fortunate they did that, as rats, hedgehogs and blackbirds in the vicinity would have eaten it all before I could scare them away.

Every morning and evening they rang the brass bell again and put out another dish of food. It was delicious and meant that if I did not manage to catch my own supper it did not matter so much. My scars began to heal. I began to put on weight and get back my full strength. My hair became glossy and softer to stroke.

I actually began to enjoy grooming myself.

Occasionally Ma had a day off work and spent the dry daylight hours weeding in the garden. She would bring out a mug of tea and enjoy a rest on a bench with me sitting companionably beside her. She would groom me and looked satisfied if she found a dead flea in her comb. 'That flea and worming medicine must have been successful. What a handsome, glossy creature you are becoming, Stripey Cat!'

Then everything changed. The snows came back again and the ground froze. Thankfully Clara and Drew insisted I was taken indoors. I was allotted a spot next to a radiator inside the kitchen porch where I was given a cat bed. But I was not allowed inside the kitchen itself, where I knew Cassie and Sofa ruled. I realised that I was becoming quite attached to all the Human Beans who lived here and I prayed that Celia would not find a new home for any of her rescue cats before the family and the kittens were able to adopt me.

The family had a consultation one evening. I could hear them as they sat after dinner chatting around the kitchen table.

'He's been here a month, now,' said Clara, 'and we haven't even given him a name!'

'Mm,' said Ma. 'Clara, when the kittens came to us from Celia's cat shelter, you named Cassie, 'Cassandra' because you said it sounded more like long, elegant piece of ribbon. And Drew, you insisted on changing Sophie's name to 'Sofa', because you thought she looked like a cuddly, soft seat. But what do you think this young fella should be named?'

'Do you think we could call him 'Tigger' like Christopher Robin's tiger in 'Winnie-the-Pooh?' Drew suggested.

'That's a good name for him,' Ma replied. 'His coat is getting glossy and smooth and he's striped like a tiger. However, I suspect he's not as courageous.'

'A brilliant name! I'm sure if we give him a name like Tigger, it will help him have more courage,' Pa responded, 'Although there's been no word from Celia, it could be that, with this warmer weather returning, she'll re-home one of her strays and he could go to her instead of staying here.'

'Oh, no!' cried Clara 'He's becoming such a handsome cat. I adore him! He's so gentle. Can we keep him? Please! Please can we keep him?'

'I would love him to sleep on my bed now he has no worms or fleas,' pleaded Drew. 'It's not fair that everyone sleeps with a cat at their feet except me! Please can he stay?'

'We need to wait and see how the kittens adapt to him,' reasoned Pa. 'We have a very special, peaceful life here. It would be sad to turn it into mayhem.'

At that point in time I had no idea what mayhem meant, but I was soon to find out.

'Half term holiday from school is coming up, so it would be sensible to let the kittens meet him when we are around to monitor their behaviour, and his,' Ma suggested. 'I'm tired of clearing out their litter trays. As soon as the snow is gone we'll allow them all out in the garden again and they can get used to each other. Whose turn is it to wash the dishes? Remember the rule.... If you cook you do not wash up.'

In some ways I am glad I am a cat and more able to wash my paws than wash dishes, but Clara and Drew knew that I liked to help with the washing up by licking clean all the plates. They smuggled them out to the porch. I was very meticulous.

CHAPTER 7

MAYHEM

A few days later, I had finished my early breakfast in the porch and was sitting tidily on the floor tiles giving myself the usual thorough wash, when suddenly the kitchen door opened. Out rushed a kitten-sized, roly-poly ball of black and white fur. She skidded to a halt with a shocked mew and then spat at me with such a venomous set of fangs that I jumped back, springing onto the porch windowsill to get out of her way. A pot plant wobbled and decided to respond in a really silly way by falling with a crash, spilling soil, leaves and flowers all over the floor. It really was being most inconsiderate. The kitten backed away into a corner, even more spooked by the noise of the pot crashing than by the sight of a striped tomcat on her territory. But Clara did not seem to mind the mess. She seemed not to see it.

'Now, now, Sofa! Don't worry about Tigger. He won't scratch you,' she soothed, picking up the kitten and attempting to cradle her. 'Try to be a polite kitten!'

But Sofa wasn't having any of it. She wriggled and struggled and scratched so badly that Clara had to drop her. I could see that Clara's wrist was bleeding, but she just sucked at it and opened the door so that Sofa could run out into the garden.

'Get rid of that monster before I'm back!' I heard the kitten order in think speak.

'Bossy paws!' I thought to myself. It was going to take a lot of patience and charm to make friends with that one.

Clara tried to calm me with her undamaged hand, but I stood rooted to the spot in alarm when a streak of black kitten skittered into the porch from the kitchen area, batting a yellow, tinkly toy along the tiles before her. She suddenly noticed me. Her eyes grew round with alarm. She stared at me as though she could not quite believe her eyes. Then, with her fur standing on end to make herself look bigger, she arched her back. She did a quick sniff of the air; did a vertical take off and then bolted back into the kitchen to hide somewhere.

Ma, who had been preparing food in the kitchen, suddenly jumped and dropped her kitchen knife as though she had been attacked at ankle level. Cassie shot past her and disappeared down a very dark, convenient, narrow passageway at the side of the Aga cooking range.

'Ma! Cassandra is hiding somewhere. She's frightened of Tigger!' shouted Clara, still sucking at her bleeding wrist.

Ma recovered her balance, wiped her hands on a towel hanging from a hook and stared at Clara. 'What's happened,

Clara? You're bleeding?'

'Sofa got frightened and wouldn't let me hold her safely. She clawed me. That's all. Just stick a plaster on it for me. It will be fine.'

'Oh no my girl, you will need that bathing properly and then we have to get you to the doctor's for a tetanus jab. Sofa's claws are not exactly germ free.'

I watched through the glass of the kitchen door as Ma bathed Clara's wrist. I could smell it was the same stinging stuff that Lady Doris had used on my wounds when she had given me TLC.

Clara winced as her mother bathed the wound, but she soon felt more comfortable when it was dried with cotton wool and had a plaster to keep out the stinging feeling.

I knew all about jabs at the vet and felt really sorry for Clara, who had to go and have one just because Sofa had been frightened by me. I realised that I was going to have to work really hard with these kittens to gain their trust and get them to like me, or I would end up locked inside Celia's cat shelter.

Pa, who had been working from home on his computer in the study, bustled Clara into the car and then drove off somewhere to get her tetanus jab. Ma tried to entice Cassandra out from behind the Aga with no success and Drew was given the job of sweeping up the mess in the porch.

'Tigger, my lad, you will have to live outside again,' sighed Ma, 'until we get these kittens more used to you. Off you go. I will put new hay in your basket in the workshop and you can sleep in there for now.'

I felt unwanted and decided to seek out my friend Liberace down at Bimblewick House, or maybe have a chat with the magpies in the lane.

However, before the bell tinkled for my food that evening, Drew and Clara paid me a special visit in the workshop. 'Poor Tiggy!' soothed Clara, stroking me gently with her undamaged hand. 'I wish the kittens were more accepting of him.'

'It's only in their nature. Cats defend their territory and protect themselves,' said Drew wistfully. 'It says so in the cat book I'm reading. I bet it's going to take a long time for all three of them to get used to each other. It can't be very comfortable for him sleeping in here when the night frost comes down. I'm going to leave my bedroom window open for him and see what happens.'

'Ma and Pa won't like your doing that without consulting them,' reasoned Clara. 'But I suppose it won't do any harm. It could be our secret.'

'Yes! Like in those mystery books we read!' whispered Drew excitedly.

Drew normally slept in a ground level extension to the cottage. I often saw him from the courtyard as he opened his bedroom blinds in the morning and began to dress. It would be easy to jump in through his bedroom window if he left it open. It sounded really inviting.

That night was utter bliss. After I had eaten outside, licked my dish and washed myself clean, I went on my usual evening patrol, looking for rodents and anything else that moved at ground level. As the night got colder and the mist came down, my fur began to fluff itself up against the cold. I felt it was time to look for the open window. Drew had remembered. He had also remembered to leave the blind raised a little so that I could get onto the windowsill inside.

As I was still quite slim, it was very easy to get through the gap and I soon homed in on his warm body. He stirred sleepily as I snuggled up close. He cradled me with his arm and I nuzzled him with my nose, as he sighed contentedly. Here was my very first, young, human friend. I was definitely getting over my prejudice against children.

The dawn woke me and called me to the garden, so that by the time the family were up and preparing for work and school there was no evidence of me in Drew's bedroom.... Apart, that is, from a few of my hairs on the bed. I was so grateful to Drew that, when I caught a rabbit later that day, I thought it would be a good idea to take it to him as a present. I hoped he liked eating dead rabbit. It was my favourite wild food and I would take extra care to take out the nasty bits he should not eat.

He had locked the bedroom window when he left for school, so I hid the dead rabbit in the workshop temporarily and did an extra spray on the dragon by the door to keep any other cats away. The dragon stared at me in disgust, but, as he wasn't really real, refused to say anything. The kittens, poor things, were locked in the cottage with their litter trays and toys. Rather them than me. I loved the freedom of the outdoors, as long as I had some sort of warm shelter when it got cold.

As soon as Drew got in from school he went into his downstairs bedroom and opened his window. He changed out of his school uniform and went into the kitchen for a snack. Now was my opportunity to give him a lovely surprise. Although the dead rabbit was almost as big as myself, I was able to drag it all the way to the open window. My jaws clamped onto its neck and I heaved. In one go, I managed to jump up and then down onto Drew's bedroom floor. I could hear Ma talking to Drew as she came into the bedroom. I scurried under the bed with my present, eager not to be detected.

'Have you any homework I can help with, Drew?'

'Not tonight, Ma! I finished my robot story in class time, so I can play with the kittens, or help get dinner ready if you like?' Drew replied.

'Cassandra is still behind the range in the kitchen and I'm frightened to poke at her with a stick in case I injure her. I've had to turn off the Aga in case she burns herself; so we will have no hot water or central heating tonight. We will have to manage with cold chicken salad and light the log burner.'

'O.K.'

'Remember to put your dirty sports kit in the laundry basket. Oh! Has Sofa been in here? Your bed is full of cat hairs.'

'I'm not sure,' Drew lied. His voice had a funny wobble as though he found telling a lie uncomfortable. He followed Ma back into the kitchen, so I thought I had better stay hidden along with my rabbit for now.

Most of the house would get cold without the central heating working the radiators, so I had a brilliant idea about sending a mind picture to Drew. Nan Knitwarm used to light her coal fire with firelighters she made from old newspapers. She would roll them up and fold them into concertina shapes. First she would unfold her old newspapers and spread them out on the floor. Then she would roll them up diagonally from the corners. This made long, long poles of newspaper before she folded them into firelighters. Surely one of those would make a wonderful tool for poking Cassandra out of the back of the Aga.

I imagined Drew rolling up the old newspapers in the kitchen and sent the mind picture to him to see if he was receptive.

I could hear he was getting a glass of milk out of the fridge, so I paused and sent the mind picture a second time, imagining the newspaper roll poking Cassandra's furry bottom. He got it this time and I could hear him saying to Ma, 'Why don't we roll up an old newspaper to make a long shaft. We can squeeze that in at the back of the Aga and tickle Cassie's bum with it.'

'What a really clever idea!' said Ma. 'It couldn't possibly hurt her.'

I could hear Clara joining in by now. She was given the job of finding some large pieces of wood in the workshop that would do to block off the sides of the Aga once they had got Cassandra out.

'I can feel it touching her,' whispered Drew. 'She's moving along. She's nearly out at the other end. Grrreat!' he eventually shouted, as I heard the scrabble of the kitten's panicky paw-skitter along the kitchen floor tiles. 'Open the kitchen door, Clara, so she can escape into the hall!'

There seemed to be a complicated plan to temporarily obstruct the narrow passages at both sides of the Aga with Clara's large blocks of wood and then to get Pa to do a permanent block-off and tiling job at some future date.

Cassandra now seemed completely unconcerned about her 'adventure.' I could hear her playing 'catch the tinkly ball' on the stairs with Drew. I could imagine the amazing game. Drew would be throwing her fluffy ball up the stairwell and, even before it had landed, she would have leapt to catch it. From my spying spot on the porch windowsill, I had seen her in action several times.... very impressive indeed. She could grab the ball from midair, twisting and arching her lithe, streamlined, little body into any shape required. Then she would bat the ball intentionally down the stairs to land at Drew's feet, staring wide-eyed at him with the command, 'THROW IT AGAIN!'

Pa jokingly insisted it was Cassie who had invented the double helix spiral shape, discovered by the DNA scientists Crick and Watson. Ma called her a 'Cirque Du Soleil' star after some famous circus act. I could tell that Sofa was really jealous of this special talent, although she had many talents of her own.

It was definitely close to evening mealtime. The Aga was restarted and the central heating turned on again. My bell was rung outside, so I went to eat from my dish and Ma closed Drew's bedroom window firmly against the cold. I hoped Drew would find my present and be ever grateful to me.

Drew and Clara had not managed to get me back inside for a couple of nights. Ma had done something with his bedroom window lock and Drew could not get the window to open more than an inch; but if I hid under the holly bush beneath his window I could hear them talking when they came in from school.

'Phwaw!' said Clara as she hung up her coat in the cloakroom area near Drew's bedroom door. 'Something smells bad in your bedroom, Drew.'

Ma went to investigate. I always suspected she had a keen sense of smell.

'Have you left some dirty football kit under the bed, Drew?' There was a dreadful pause as she bent towards the direction of the smell. 'Oh no! There's a dead rabbit under your bed. It must have been here a couple of days. It really pongs. It's too big for Cassie and Sofa to have dragged in. A present from Tigger Digger I do believe!'

With that Ma marched outside and hunted me down. It did not take her long to discover me skulking behind Dragon in the workshop. He was absolutely useless at coming to my defence, no matter how fiercely he stared.

Ma grabbed hold of me by the loose fur at the back of my neck and took me inside to present me to the dead rabbit. It did not look impressed, but was glad that she had no plans to cook it for dinner.

The glow of her bean-shaped light was very cross indeed as she pushed me towards the smelly carcass. She tapped my nose sharply making it sting. Then I nearly jumped out of my fur as she yelled, 'NO!'

I was pushed out into the cold evening air with my ears humming and my nose very much the worse for wear.

I think I got her message. Human Beans do not appreciate presents, no matter how tasty. I thought that maybe I had made the biggest mistake ever and that would be the end of my stay at the cottage.

However, later that evening, as the family settled down to their own dinner, I heard my bell ring and a bowl of food miraculously appeared outside the kitchen door. They had forgiven me.

Ma came back from shopping one day with a curiously magical thing that she plugged into the porch electrical socket. Once it was plugged in, she allowed me back into the porch. It sent out a smell that reminded me of my mother and seemed very reassuring. I perched on the inside of the porch windowsill and sunned myself in the spring sunshine. Inhaling the smell, I began to relax and drifted off to sleep.

Miraculously it seemed to have a

similar effect on the kittens. Later that morning, Ma let them out of the kitchen through to the porch. They noticed me, but did not do their usual thing of hissing and arching their backs with fangs at the ready. Their noses twitched and, although they still looked suspicious of me, they did not back away. Sofa was the more confident kitten and rubbed against the legs of the circular porch table, just to prove she was in control of the situation. Cassandra held back and hid herself behind a cane chair, deciding to watch proceedings before daring to run for the door. The porch table held a new pot of geraniums, which for a moment wobbled dangerously. In the end it gave in and decided to cooperate. It settled and seemed to smile.

'I suppose we could use the table as a roundabout,' mewed Sofa in her best film star voice. 'That way we do not need to meet nose to nose as we come and go from the house.'

'Good idea, Sofa' Cassandra agreed. 'Tigger doesn't look too dangerous a fiend this morning. I know he sent the family a mind picture with an idea of how to rescue me from behind the Aga. I suppose that was kind and shows he cares about me. I think I will risk a run past him onto the lawn.' With that she sprinted around the other side of the roundabout table and streaked out into the garden.

Sofa took everything a bit more leisurely, fixing me with a stare that seemed to say, 'Don't you dare move...! Especially as I am about to make my theatrical exit!'

With that she flounced out past the roundabout table and paused with her nose in the air, before tiptoeing and sashaying along the hosepipe that Ma had stretched down the full length of the garden path. She was trying to avoid her paws touching the sharp gravel. She held her tail aloft to help her balance, demonstrating the daring of a tightrope walker as she wiggled her plump little body along the length of the hosepipe. She made me smile and twitch my whiskers. *Inkstink* told me that Human Beans enjoyed this type of fur-coat modelling. They even call it 'sashaying along a catwalk.'

CHAPTER 8

BONDING

Things began to settle down into a routine. I was allowed into Drew's bedroom, once I had been groomed and checked for fleas. Pa suggested that Drew monitored my going in and out of the bedroom window very carefully and was not to encourage my bringing him dead presents. The bedroom window was only to be opened wide when Drew was in charge. That suited me. I could get into his bedroom for a nap if I mewed outside. I would not bring him any more dead presents. Perhaps Human Beans liked live things. I would try that instead.

Drew was reading in his bedroom one

evening when I turned up with a pretty vole. She was wriggling in my mouth, so I sort of made a peculiar strangled mew that got Drew to the window. He was getting the hang of sending mind-messages. When he saw the vole he said 'Drop it!' and at the same time sent a picture of my doing it. I did as I was told. Then he praised me, calling me a 'Good boy' and opened the window wide for me. For a moment I was tempted to follow my *instink* which told me to run after the scampering vole, but I was really more interested in getting warm and away from the chill spring evening.

I was getting better at reading Drew's mind pictures too. I knew he was busy praying and asking the Great Light to love and protect all his family. My heart melted a little, as I saw him include the kittens and me in his thoughts about his family circle. I had had a lovely home with Nan Knitwarm, but I had never been part of a family before. It felt very special indeed.

Drew finished his prayer. Then we

had a warm snuggle together on the bed whilst he read a book about climate change for his homework. I crouched contentedly, purring very loudly. I could hear Ma singing in the kitchen as she prepared the evening meal. I could hear Clara's voice too, as she helped entertain the kittens by teasing them with a piece of string. She kept wiggling it for them and chortled every time they chased it. They obviously thought it was some sort of prey for them to hunt.

'It's a bit strange that Tigger never wants to join in any of the kittens' play,' said Clara. 'I'm sure the kittens would let him now they are used to his being around.'

'Maybe he was never really taught to play by his mother. Perhaps he left her side too soon to learn about how important playing is. Pretending to be grown up is a way of practising for becoming adult. It's a very important stage in everyone's life, especially for animals,' said Ma stirring a pot of fragrant, vegetable curry.

'I suppose it makes them strong and able to catch their own food in the wild,' said Clara thoughtfully, whilst she whizzed a ribbon around in a tantalising circle for Sofa. I could imagine the kitten following its path with her nose; then becoming very dizzy, getting cross-eyed and falling over herself. She could never resist anything stringy that moved.

'It makes me feel so sad that he left his mother too soon; but it makes me even sadder to think that someone would dump him out on the moors to fend for himself.'

'You're right, Clara. There are cruel and thoughtless people in the world, but fortunately I would say from my experience that most people are really kind.'

I could hear Clara beginning to get our stainless steel cat dishes ready for our dinner. They clattered as she washed them, making them really clean before filling them with our evening meals. I decided it was time to jump down off Drew's bed and saunter into the kitchen, pretending I had not been listening.

'Thanks, Clara, for feeding the cats,' said Ma. 'They're less likely to pester for food whilst we're eating if their stomachs are full.'

'Tigger's never full. I think he was so used to going hungry when he was a wild cat, he wants to stock up in case we dump him on the moors,' Drew observed as he came into the kitchen enticed by the smell of his own dinner. Just like me really.'

'I love the way he begs by sitting with both white paws neatly together, then lifts then one paw at a time,' said Clara, mimicking me. 'His eyes are so appealing. They're like big pools that home in on you and make it hard to say no to him. He's just making sure we know how handsome he is.'

I had rarely been called 'handsome' before. It made me feel very grown up and quite noble. I thought I had better behave responsibly and not attempt to jump onto the dinner table. It was my job to show Cassandra and Sofa how to behave. After all, I am so much older and wiser. I had finished my supper, so sat licking myself clean near the warmth of the Aga, listening to the family as they ate.

'That's a lovely prayer you were chanting Ma,' said Clara encouragingly.

'Thank you my lovely. I was just trying to remember all the words. I think I will put it into the devotional at the beginning of our feast tomorrow night.'

'Will there be lots of people coming to feast tomorrow?' Clara asked. 'I could help you with some cleaning tonight and Drew could make his apple scones to serve with tea afterwards.

'That would be a great help Clara. I think there will be about twenty of us including the children. At the nineteen-day feast we will just have tea and biscuits and whatever savoury snacks you children would like. I've organised a potluck buffet for your party on Sunday, so we only need to do a little food preparation for that. Samir said he would bring pizza and Helena some

Persian rice. All the Bahá'ís coming have promised to bring a food contribution for that, so all we have to do is make sure the kitchen table is set out with cutlery, plates and napkins.'

Oh, a feast for 19 days AND a big party! That sounded wonderful, I thought. There is usually some left over chicken from parties and feasting. These Bahá'ís, whoever they are, must be gluttons with all that eating. However, I'm not so keen on lots of Human Beans having their party feet so close to me. It's a trodden paw accident waiting to happen. I was thinking I might hide behind the sofa or under a bed until leftovers time.

'What feast is it tomorrow night, Ma?' asked Clara. 'I can never remember the names of them all.'

'Well as you know there are nineteen feasts throughout the Bahá'í year and one happens every nineteen days,' Ma explained.

Oops ! Oh dear. How disappointing, I thought to myself. I got that totally wrong. I had imagined a party lasting nineteen days long. It was really just one day in every nineteen.

'Each one of them is named after a quality of God. The title of tomorrow's feast is 'Jalál' and that means 'Glory'. I suppose it tells us something of the power and light God brings to our lives,' said Pa joining in the conversation whilst scraping his dinner plate clean.

'Mmmm. That word 'glory' seems glowing and warm, just like God's love wrapping all around us,' said Clara thoughtfully,

'You always say such insightful things, Clara. I hope you won't be shy when we're consulting and discussing together at our feast. You always have such creative ideas.'

I noticed that Clara's glow all around her Human Bean shape got bigger when Pa praised her like that. I thought maybe it would be a good thing for me to copy. If I praised the kittens when they were behaving well, then maybe their behaviour would improve.

What an interesting day it had been. It had begun with Pa getting up very early in order to do some work in his study before the family made the house too noisy. He had shuffled sleepily into the bathroom and did not bother to shut the door as no one else was around... apart from me, that is.

I was busy watching the early birds from my favourite spy-spot on the landing windowsill. I jumped down and sauntered into the bathroom where Pa was sitting on the toilet with his hair standing on end and his tartan pyjama trousers rumpled around his ankles. He reminded me of a toilet brush stuck upside down in a toilet pan. I pretended not to look at him, as he might have been embarrassed. I hate it if anyone catches me going to the toilet, especially if they tell me off for digging a very deep hole.

Pa yawned sleepily and did not seem to bother as I climbed right inside his crumpled pyjama trousers where I discovered a lovely fleecy, warm patch. I looked at the door to check no one else was coming and started to snuggle down; but Pa started chortling when my paws got stuck in his waist elastic and I began riding up and down like a yo-yo.

'First time I've ever seen a cat bungee jumping,' he snorted. He could not resist picking me up and giving me a snuggle. I knew it was his way of saying I was now a fully-fledged member of the family, but I wish he had waited until he had shaved. His cheeks were as prickly as a hedgehog!

It was a crisp bright morning when Ma drove the children to the school bus, whilst Pa settled down in the study to work on his computer. Normally Sofa would have stayed to help him write, occasionally tapping the keyboard to make him shout. She would often rub up against his face to remind him it was time to put the kettle on and give her a fuss. But Ma had decided that it was time to let the kittens out to wander in the garden, especially as I was around to keep an eye on them.

'Out you go for some fresh air until I get back!' Ma instructed the kittens, patting their bottoms and guiding them onto the lawn. 'I won't be long. Tigger Digger you are in charge. Look after your little sisters.' I waved my tail as Clara and Drew got into the car and Ma drove them away.

'I'm really excited about exploring!' mewed Sofa. 'The big wide world is out there and I want to discover it!'

'Don't go far, Sofa. You could be in danger. There are wild cats further afield and a fox. They will not be as friendly as Thunder. There is farm traffic on the lane too. You might get squashed like cow manure.'

'As if!' she retorted as she made her way confidently down the front path into the lane. 'I'll be careful!'

Cassie wasn't so sure about the big wide world and rarely strayed further than saying good morning to Dragon and sniffing around the lavender bushes. 'I'm feeling a bit dithery about exploring, Tigger. Will you come with me?'

'Of course I will, young lady. I will follow. You lead the way.'

Cassie was interested in sniffing at every flower and mouse trail she came across. It was extremely tedious for an active fella like myself. The only drama was when she arched her back and fluffed out her fur, snarling with her fangs to demonstrate to Dragon that she was a fearsome force to be contended with.

Just then I heard a roar of an engine and a great squeal of breaks from the lane. 'Cassie. Stay here by Dragon. Don't move until I get back!'

I ran as fast as my four legs would carry me, expecting to see a 'squashed as a cow pat' kitten in the lane.

'Don't know what all the fuss is about,' said a voice from the top of the old mounting-block, where Sofa sat licking one paw nonchalantly. 'He shouted at me and waved his fists. Had plenty of time to stop.' She continued licking herself, determined not to show that she had frightened herself to a frazzle.

I could see a very large truck full of sheep, rocking from side to side and being transported at a very gentle speed along the lane towards Spud and Chip's old farm.

'You must have given that driver such a turn, Sofa, and all the sheep will be in shock after he had to do an emergency stop. What did you think was clever about running across the road in front of a truck? You know from watching out of the window how dangerous it can be!'

'I judged the distance very carefully,' she answered. 'I ran in between the space I could see after the front wheels and before the back ones.'

I gasped. I was shocked and angry now at the risk she had taken. No wonder Human Beans talk about cats having nine lives. 'Well not well enough! Everything we do has consequences. Thought you just might have learned that lesson by now!'

'Do you think that is one of my nine lives lost?'

'Probably. And when you wove in and out between Ragnar's feet the other day, that was probably one as well.'

'I was perfectly safe. Didn't you hear Mrs. Thwackit tell Clara that horses freeze when they feel something rubbing against their legs. They think it's a snake and it's an *inkstink* response.'

'That sounds a bit fur-fetched to me,' I said. You must be more careful in the future. Come on! Let's find Cassie!'

But Cassie was nowhere to be seen. Dragon was sitting alone by the workshop door looking glum and dumb.... 'Neither use, nor ornament!' as Nan Knitwarm would have said.

Fortunately with Sofa's help I was able to pick up Cassie's scent trail, as we squeezed through the prickly hawthorn hedge into the meadow beyond the garden. She was nowhere to be seen and I had an awful feeling of dread in the pit of my stomach. I knew she was in danger. She was ignoring my frantic mind pictures.

We skirted the meadow full of young thistles and buttercups and came across a drystone wall where we could scent her paw trail. She had definitely jumped up onto the wall. I jumped up easily, but Sofa was too roly-poly pudding-like to attempt it. I told her to run along the base of the wall and get into the next field under a five-barred gate that I could see in the distance.

Nothing black and furry came into view, only huge cattle snuffling around in the grass. 'Seen a black, scrawny kitten?' I messaged to the cattle.

'Probably gone to drink in the stream down in the valley,' messaged a great towering bull, who seemed to be in charge of his herd.

We scampered as fast as our paws could carry us to the bottom of the field, where hidden from view was a winding stream with steep banks. The water gurgled along and so did something else. A streak of something black was struggling to get up a steep muddy bank and failing miserably.

She was unrecognizable. Her thin, black coat was dripping with mud and plastered against her tiny body. She looked half her size and pitifully weak. Any moment now and she would lose her battle, slither back into the water and drown.

I noticed a thick log of wood close by the bank and thought-messaged Sofa to help me push it towards the stream. If we could get it lodged between the bank and the water she would have something to hold on to with her claws and so would we. We worked urgently and scrabbled with our paws until we got it rolling down to the water. It fell with a splosh into the streambed, making a sort of bridge. If only she could manage to get to that, I thought. Great Light of Heaven help us!

To our relief in a just few moments she was grappling with her claws onto the end of the log. If I could only balance as well as Sofa could, I would be able to teeter along the log and grab Cassie by her neck before she went under again. She was far too weak to haul her own body out of the water.

'Hold on Cassie. Keep still now whilst we rescue you!' The log wobbled dangerously when I first began to crawl out to her; but I found if I crouched low I sort of became part of the log and it stopped bobbing about so much. The worst bit was when I grabbed at her loose fur behind her neck. It was very hard not to hurt her, but she was too frightened to squeak. At last we had her on the grassy bank and were able to roll her dry a little and lick her warm.

'One of your nine lives gone, Cassie,' said Sofa unsympathetically.

'No need to rub it in, Sofa. Just keep rubbing Cassie until she gets warm. Then I will carry her home.'

It was trickier than I imagined. Cassie was unable to walk. She was so shivery and weak, but I managed to pick her up by the scruff of her neck and, if I trotted very tall indeed, could carry her along with her feet dragging a little in the grass. The herd of cattle was very curious and came for a look at us. Sofa hissed at them and grew twice her size to frighten them away. Fortunately they turned tail and went to graze at the other side of the field.

It would be hard to jump up on top of the wall with her in my mouth, so we had to go the long way round under the wooden gate. My shoulders ached, but *inkstink* told me it was urgent to take Cassandra back home to get her warm and dry.

Every time I needed a little rest, Sofa would snuggle up to Cassie and lick her reassuringly, until I found the strength to carry on. It was good but tedious teamwork.

We arrived home at last by the kitchen door and needed to make ourselves heard. Pa would be at the front of the cottage in his study and would not hear a mew from the kitchen door. I contemplated jumping at the hanging brass bell; but instead decided to tell Sofa to go round the front of the cottage and alert Pa by mewing on the study windowsill.

Pa soon got the message when Sofa's plump little body cut out the daylight to his computer. He tried to let her in at the window, but gave up when she scampered round towards the kitchen door.

'Oh what a bedraggled, wet kitten,' said Pa. 'Whatever happened to you? I see that Tigger Digger brought you back home safely. Well done, young chap. Let's get Miss Cassandra in a warm bath and blow dry her.'

'Oh no!' thought Cassie. 'Not that!'

Ma always seemed to have good ideas. She was tired of shouting at Thunder, the dog from the Thwackits. He was very lonely during the day and often sought friendship with any Human Bean willing to pay him attention. Unfortunately, he thought the best way into the cottage garden was to jump over the hedge and land kerplonk onto the flowerbed. Ma was not impressed, especially as she had planted a swathe of brightly coloured spring bulbs and Thunder had smashed half of them down.

She decided to spray him with water from the hosepipe every time he jumped over the hedge; but praise and stroke him whenever he chose to use the gate. Third time lucky! He soon got the message. He did not enjoy being sprayed with bitterly cold water. However, he did enjoy coming through the gate and getting fussed. Ma had left the hosepipe spread out along the gravel path just to remind him; so Sofa took advantage of it and did her catwalk thing, sashaying along the hosepipe like a seasoned tightrope walker.

'I'm such a pretty paws!' she said as she congratulated herself for avoiding the sharp gravel.

'Glamour puss,' woofed Thunder.

I was very nervous when Thunder first started coming into the garden. I remembered how he had tried to run me off his territory with his loud barking;

but, once Ma was there to supervise, fuss and encourage him, he seemed to accept me as part of the family set up. Sofa and Cassandra started to put up with me too and we all enjoyed being fussed, petted and having the occasional treat of cat biscuits.

The vet had told us that Sofa needed to strengthen her heart and lose some weight. She needed daily exercise; so Ma suggested that Drew and Clara take it in turns to lead the kittens up the public footpath beyond the cottage. They took advantage of the school holidays and set off each day as the sun began to warm the fields. Thunder very quickly decided he wanted to join in and soon there was a trail of small Human Beans and animals walking along the footpath, jumping through the tall grasses and up over the stile to the field beyond. I was very curious indeed and decided to follow. Since my rescue of Cassie, the kittens had been really friendly. Occasionally they even allowed me to make a threesome, sitting by the fire of a chilly evening.

Clara led the way on the first day, along the footpath by Ragnar's field and over the stile into the cow pasture. At first the cows stirred in fright when they saw three cats along with a hunting dog; but they soon settled down to munching the grass again, once Clara reassured them. I was still a touch nervous about the whole escapade, especially being near to Thunder; so I padded quietly along observing. Sofa and Cassie, however, enjoyed every bound over the tall grass and enthusiastically played hide-and-seek all along the route. Then they would run joyful, helter-skelter circles around Thunder until he collapsed panting. He was too old for this lark. It made him dizzy just trying to keep track of them.

One bright morning was particularly noisy. The curlews had arrived on the moors to make their nests and breed, shortly followed by the lapwings. They were courting and nesting ready to rear their young. Drew had decided we would go along the public footpath and take a picnic, so that we could sit on the stile and look out over towards the reservoirs and the woods.

One male curlew was very worried. He could see our little band wending its way towards the holly thicket, where he and his mate had made a nest and she was brooding some eggs. Cats and a dog were seen as predators and children with loud voices were definitely unwelcome. There was no sweet haunting trill, but an angry alarm call as he swooped and dived at us with his curved beak, trying to drive us away.

'It's a terror-dactile,' cried Drew dramatically as he dodged the attack. 'I've seen them in my dinosaur book!'

'You are right it does look a bit like a pterodactyl, Drew, but they're extinct now you know. It's a curlew. He's terrified we'll discover his young in the nest. Let's take the kittens over the stile into the meadow. We could hide behind the drystone wall,' Clara suggested as she herded us along. We ducked our heads against the swooping creature as he gave a final bat at us with his wings and swooped angrily away.

The six of us finally landed on the other side of the stile and were relieved to find the field empty of cattle. Drew had brought his eyenoculars and Clara had stuffed her backpack with tasty snacks. We settled down in the long grass and Thunder made a good cushion for Clara to lean against. We lazed and snacked, licked and nuzzled. Drew used his eynoculars with great enthusiasm.

'Look! There's another curlew with its curved beak. And look down in the fields below. I can spot some lapwings. They've got shivery crowns like Liberace,' crooned Drew.

'They've got that lovely green and blue, iridescent plumage too,' added Clara.

'Ooh, a little blue van has stopped near Lord Bimblewick's gate. A man is getting out. Maybe he's got a delivery?'

'Here, let me see,' said Clara taking the eyenoculars. 'No, he's not delivering anything. He's taking the capstones off the wall and putting them in his van. The back of the van is getting lower and lower the more he piles in.'

'Let's run back and tell Ma. She can phone for the police,' suggested Drew, already setting off home.

I could see all this activity with my eyes. I did not need eyenoculars. First I recognised the van and then I recognised the man. It was Noddle Nephew Newton. He was stealing the capstones off the wall, heaving them all into his van. Risking stealing in broad daylight was not a very bright thing to do, but maybe he thought that Lord Bimblewick was too busy polishing his Humber Hawk to notice.

'We must try to remember the number plate on the van,' said Clara. 'The police can trace the owner through the number plate registered. They'll find out who is doing the stealing.'

I could see the number plate clearly. It said 'NODL 123Z'

Clara and Drew began to run back

towards the cottage and Thunder and the kittens thought it an amazing game of chase. I followed, fixing the memory of the registration plate in my mind's eye. 'NODL 123Z'

'Ma!' cried Drew as he burst breathlessly into the kitchen followed by the whole gang. 'Phone the police! There's a man with a van stealing Lord Bimblewick's capstones off his drystone wall!'

Ma ran out into the lane; but by that time the van had groaned away with its heavy load, the drystone wall was bare of its capstones. The wall had already started to crumble down in weak places. It looked very forlorn.

'Can you remember the registration number on the van?' Ma asked.

'Yes it was DODL 123Z', said Drew.

'No it was YODL 132Z' said Clara.

I sent an urgent mind picture to both of them with the correct image of the number. They both looked at each other then suddenly chanted the correct number in unison, 'NODL 123Z!'

Ma was soon on the telephone to the police with the registration number and they thanked us for being so co-operative with our crime detecting. They promised to send someone round to take a statement.

'How did you do that?' said Sofa admiring my ability to transfer my mind picture.

'We all have that ability, Sofa. We send mind pictures to each other all the time. We did it before we developed any sort of cat language. Human Beans did it better before they invented speech. The more you practise the better you get.' I sounded very wise, but really I was just repeating something Chip had once told me.

'You are clever, Tigger,' said Cassandra, looking at me with new eyes.... not her usual unfriendly ones.

Later that day, after Lord Bimblewick

had been told about the theft of his capstones and Lady Doris's pink bunny slippers had got rather wobbly and agitated, Thunder started barking. A yellow and white police car drew up in the lane with a flashing blue light on the top. Clara and Drew were fascinated as they looked out of the front kitchen window. Sofa jumped up on the windowsill in her usual curious way but Cassie got frightened by the flashing light and tried to hide behind the Aga again. Ma picked her up and soothed her. Two police officers got out of the police car and wandered down the lane to inspect the damage to the walling. Lord Bimblewick came out and invited them into Bimblewick House, but they declined and said they needed to talk to the children first.

Ma was already at the kitchen door with Cassie in her arms as they arrived and welcomed them both inside. She seemed to know one of the officers as she laughed and invited them both to sit down. 'Would you like a cup of tea,

Officer Darling?'

I had heard Ma call Pa 'Darling' before and sometimes Clara and Drew, but never someone outside the family. He must be very dear friend indeed.

'This is P.C. Darling, Drew. He came and helped me to rescue Henry from being walled up that time. You were just a baby then, but Clara will remember.'

'Yes, you were demolishing some old walling in the old stable and came across a red canister hiding in the wall cavity. You were really frightened, Ma. You thought it was a bomb and called the police!'

'I remember it well,' said P.C. Darling. 'It was my first investigation after I had passed my police exams and I came up to take a look in case it was something serious. I remember deciding to take a sledgehammer to the wall. As I swung it I noticed two large eyes looking at me from the wall cavity. I carried on with my demolition and eventually helped a very old Henry vacuum cleaner escape from the wall. It was made of red metal and had two very large black and white, artwork eyes on its face. It didn't work. More's the pity. Someone must have decided long ago that it wasn't worth taking to the tip, so they used it to fill in a gap in the wall. I was the laughing stock of the police station and they have never let me live it down. I am always being teased about that dangerous criminal, Henry!'

The other police officer cleared his throat as a signal that maybe we were wasting police time 'Well the thief who took the capstones is not necessarily a dangerous criminal, but it is so annoying and a very skilled and costly business to repair the walls. All the drystone walling will disintegrate the more people steal the capstones for their garden walls. Who was the first person to notice the thief?'

'It was me,' said Drew. 'I was bird spotting with my binoculars and noticed something odd. Then Clara looked through them and tried to read the registration number of the van.'

'I sent 'NODL 123Z" to them both in a mind picture and they chanted it together, as though I was conducting them in a choir.

'NODL 123Z! Definitely NODL 123Z!'

'Well done!' said the second police officer. P.C. Darling was busy writing everything down in his notebook as they described the van's getting heavier and heavier with its extra load. They also described Noddle Nephew Newton; but they forgot to mention that he smelled of old sausage and black pudding. Maybe he was too far away for them to have smelled it. But I had. I sent a smell message to everyone. I tried to make it very strong, but only Cassandra picked it up. I noticed she did not like the smell either and unsuccessfully tried to scramble behind the Aga again.

CHAPTER 9

THE PARTY

The nineteen-day feast, that really only lasted one evening, was crowded with lots of chatty people huddling into the cottage sitting room. Several people sat on cushions on the floor once the chairs ran out. Cassandra flew upstairs in her usual nervous, skittering way to hide under a bed; but Sofa, confident as usual, enjoyed the children fussing and stroking her. I decided, curious as ever, to hide behind the sofa and listen to find out what a Bahá'í nineteen-day feast was really all about.

It began with some soothing recorded music and that helped everyone become calm and focused. I squatted behind the biggest sofa on the carpeted bit of the flagstone floor and relished the warmth and quiet. I could just glimpse the flames from the log fire flickering and glowing from my stakeout. Even my whiskers relaxed as my eyes closed blissfully. The chatting stilled and Pa welcomed everyone to the feast of Glory. Even Drew, I could sense, had stopped twizzling his hair and the lady jiggling her baby on her lap stilled and soothed her little one. The small children, who had fussed Sofa, helped settle her on someone's lap and I recognised the prayer that Ma had been practising. What surprised me was that it was Clara who chose to sing it. I couldn't help feeling proud of my family connections. What an amazingly clear and lovely voice she had.... quite angelic and quite purrfect! I sent her a thought of encouragement and a mind picture of my giving her an approving nose nuzzle.

Then a gentleman began chanting something in a language I did not recognise. However, his love for the Light of Heaven in his thought patterns transmitted itself to me. It soothed me and I found myself drifting off to sleep, my head supported on my front paws and my whiskers enjoying a purrfect sense of security.

Suddenly I woke up as the room started buzzing with voices. It was time to discuss local matters. What I liked was that even the children were asked their opinions. I decided I must remember that the next time the kittens and I consulted together. As the eldest cat in the house, I must remember to include them in the decision-making. *Inkstink* told me it might help them to become wiser.

I gathered that a party was going to happen at the cottage on the Sunday afternoon in two days time and needed careful planning. The children had this idea of a World Citizenship party to celebrate Human Beans being one big world family. They begged to have a tree inside, so that they could hang decorations of people, animals, flowers and butterflies on it. Pa said he could bring a potted, evergreen yew tree indoors that they could use. The idea was that the party guests could write promises on some paper leaves and hang them on the tree.

Maya was a young, attractive dark-skinned lady with curly hair. She smiled. I could tell she was looking forward to helping the children make their decorations after the community had finished consulting.

Clara volunteered to make paper leaves and thread them with cotton. I could just imagine Sofa, Cassandra and myself helping with that.... Great fun in store!

Planning the party got everyone excited. Invitations had already gone out several weeks ago and it looked as though there would be a good gathering of both adults and children. They decided what prayers they would chant, what songs they would sing, what food they would bring and of course the children eagerly suggested what games they wanted to play.

Someone called Phil kindly offered to come and clean out the workshop the next day so the children would be able to have their games in a dry area if it rained. Otherwise the games would be on the lawn. Oops. Dragon would not be very pleased about being disturbed. He was always scowling anyway, so no surprises there.

Before the discussion finished and the refreshments were served, Pa asked everyone if there was any other business. Ma said that she had invited a policeman and his family to the party and also an elderly lady whom they were thinking of adopting as an extra Granny.

Ma explained that, at the care home where she ran her music and movement class, they had a scheme where visitors could adopt a granny or grandad. The old people who lived in the care home got out so rarely. The idea was that adopting a grandparent meant you took that person out on a regular basis, or visited them when they were unwell. She was keen for other people at the nineteen-day feast to perhaps do the same. Clara said she was excited and couldn't wait to meet this new grandma, as her own grandmothers lived such a long, long way away. Several people said they would think about joining the scheme.

The consulting together seemed to finish and people started moving into the kitchen area to grab a snack and a drink. The children seemed keener on dragging Maya into Drew's downstairs bedroom to make the promised tree decorations.

I felt it high time to run upstairs out of harms way and tell Cassie all about the nineteen-day feast she had missed. I was not sure she would look forward to the boisterous noise of the party everyone had planned. Maybe if I were lucky, she would allow me to snuggle up next to her on Clara's bed in the moonlight streaming through the casement window.

I could not believe the burst of activity

as the morning of the party arrived. It was as though my family had gone completely honkers bonkers, including Sofa and Cassie.

To begin with we three cats sat politely waiting for our breakfast in the kitchen. Sofa was doing her usual thing of mewing silently and using her eyes to home in on any Human Bean looking her way; but for once her magic was not working. I did my pretty-paws begging act, lifting one front paw after the other, but nobody noticed. Cassie got impatient and started rubbing and weaving round Pa's legs without the usual results. He was moving furniture around and had no patience with being tripped up.

Ma was busy making porridge, which she said would fortify everyone. It smelled revolting to me and I was not sure what 'fortify' meant, except that it did not include giving us our breakfast. It was as though we did not exist!

Clara and Drew were falling over each other, putting up balloons and streamers they had made and were fussing about how to make the sitting room more colourful. Unable to resist, both Cassie and Sofa abandoned the kitchen and immediately pounced after the trailing streamers, tripping up Pa on the way. I heard his thoughts as he recovered his balance. Not repeatable! Instead he just shouted, 'Take care! Will you?'

The previous day Pa had helped them bring in the small yew tree in its pot. They had lifted it onto the dresser in the sitting room; then decorated it with cardboard cutouts of faces of peoples from all over the world. Then they added the creatures, animals and flowers that the children had made out of card at the nineteen-day feast. The artificial paper leaves that Clara had cut out last night were ready to give to guests on their arrival. They could write their promises on them and hang them by cotton threads onto the World Citizen tree.

My stomach did a terrible rumble, so I thought it was high time for real action and let out one of my loud, insistent wails. It had the desired effect of stopping everyone in their tracks. It reminded them all that we cats needed our breakfast.

'I'm not sure what we should do with the cats during the celebrations?' queried Ma. Some people don't like cats. Maybe we should shut them in a bedroom with some food and a litter tray?'

'Aw Ma, they are our family. They should be here enjoying all the fun,' Drew complained. 'At least let them be here for the quiet devotional part of the party and then if everything gets too much for them we can shut them away. There is only one lady who is frightened of cats and she may not come.'

'That's true, Drew. She may well be visiting her family. We will have to see what happens.'

'I'll look after Cassie and soothe her during the devotional, so she doesn't get scared of so many feet,' Clara offered. And whose lap would I sit on, I wondered?

I had noticed that when I went out for my early trip to the garden the workshop had been swept and balloons and bunting put up in there too. Dragon was on duty as a doorstop and looked rather important, sitting claws together. His eyes bulged like black grapes and the green ribbon tied around his neck seemed to make him sit more upright than usual. His job was to keep the door ajar so that you could see right inside.

There was a big parcel hanging from one of the beams that looked like a giant, multicoloured wasps' nest. I wondered why it was there? There was plenty of room for the children to run around inside and I thought that later on I might jump up on one of the low beams and watch their games in absolute safety.

For some reason Clara gave us all extra rations when she finally got around to serving our breakfast. Perhaps she thought it would make us sleepy and less likely to get under people's feet.

'Gourmet food for a special day,' she whispered as she tickled my ears. 'Enjoy your treat! That word 'gourmet' again. I have never as yet met the mysterious gourmet and fancied it was some fat, juicy creature like the haggis that Pa was always joking about. Apparently it has two shorter legs on one side of its little dumpy body, so that it can run clockwise around mountains without toppling head-over-heels. The mind boggles. Maybe a gourmet is a boggle? Maybe it is totally imaginary?

There seemed to be lots of frenzied, last minute activity to prepare for the party. The bathroom and kitchen were sprayed with something I did not like the smell of; so I took a turn in the garden to freshen my nose. These Human Beans really do not know how to leave good messages.

Clara and Ma changed into new garments I had not seen before. So, as soon as I saw them come out onto the lawn all prettied up for the party, I thought I had better rub around them and help them smell more normal. They didn't seem to mind my weaving around their skirts and rubbing my cheeks on them. Pa and Drew had on their best jeans and shirts, but smelled quite normal in comparison, so I did not feel the need to odourize them.

Cars began to draw up and park outside in the lane. I could hear people's excited voices. I jumped up onto the mounting block. From there I climbed up onto the roof of the workshop to get a bird's eye view as everyone arrived. Most of the people I had met at the 19 day feast had returned; Maya and her family; the foreign gentleman with the deep voice with his family and Phil who had cleared out the workshop with his. I spotted the familiar face of P.C. Darling holding the hand of a little boy, followed by a smiling wife holding a baby. Then I smelled something very familiar.... lavender!

My eyes began to water at the memory of Nan Knitwarm's scent. My stomach gave a lurch as a gentleman helped a struggling, elderly lady out of the front seat of a minibus. My family advanced on the people arriving, hugging and greeting them and Drew and Clara were introduced to the lady with snow-white hair.

'This is Mrs. Knitwarm,' said Ma. She's our 'adopted granny'. She'll be coming to visit with us once a fortnight.'

'You can call me Nan,' Nan Knitwarm chuckled, her eyes dancing with warmth at the sight of Clara and Drew. 'All the children in my street used to call me that.'

'Come in and sit down,' Ma suggested, guiding her into the cottage, as Nan shuffled along pushing a wheelie-walker in front of her to help her balance.

I could not believe it. Nan Knitwarm was really here. The person who had homed me when I first left my mother's side was in my new home. The Human Bean, whom I had loved most in all the world was really here. I thanked the Light of Heaven and prayed she would recognize me.

Everyone was welcomed. Their coats were taken and the grown ups seated in the sitting room. The children were so excited. They gathered around the tree that Drew and Clara had dressed with all the colourful decorations they had made at the feast. There were faces of people from many different countries, cut out animals and flowers, and labels describing ideas that would make the world a safer place such as equality, justice, truthfulness and peace.

It was noisy so Cassie had made an early exit, but Clara had found her under Pa's desk in the study and brought her out to reassure her that she was safe.

She stroked her to calm her then sat down on a cushion near the fire to help her join in the special occasion.

'My what a lovely kitten you have there,' said Nan Knitwarm from the great big armchair she sat in. 'I love cats so much. I had a lovely handsome one called Tigger, but he ran away when I was taken to hospital.'

'We have a cat we call Tigger,' said

Drew. 'He was dumped on the moors and was living wild when we rescued him.'

'Here comes the fella himself,' Pa announced. I decided to walk into the middle of the room with my tail held high, so that everyone could see what a handsome cat I had grown into.

'Oh he looks so much like my Tigger,' squealed Nan. 'Might it be him I wonder?'

I did not wait a moment longer to allow her to wonder. I ran to her side, looked meaningfully up into her eyes, then jumped straight on her lap to settle myself down.

She hugged me too tightly for a moment, but then set about adoring me, rubbing my head gently and fondling my chin and ears. Tears began to slide down her cheeks. 'It is him. I'm sure of it.' She took her lavender scented handkerchief out of her handbag and wiped away her tears with a big sniffle. 'Oh I had given up hope of ever seeing him again.'

'Will you need to take him home with you?' asked Drew anxiously, worried he would no longer have a cat to call his own.

She blew her bulbous nose. 'Sadly pets are not allowed to stay in the care home where I live. They're only allowed to visit. Anyway, Drew, it would be selfish of me to take him away from such a loving family when I can't really look after him any longer. I can see he's happy and content here.' She stroked me down the length of my glossy coat and I purred loudly in response to show I agreed with her. I loved my new family and I loved my new home. And if it were still possible to occasionally sit upon the knee I adored, then that would be cat heaven as far as I was concerned.

'How strange that he should end up here with us, after we'd just decided to adopt you as our grandma,' said Ma.

'I don't think it's strange,' said Clara. 'It's just the answer to Tigger's prayers.'

'You may well be right, Clara,' Pa agreed. Prayers are extra strong wishes and carry great power. So, shall we all settle down and begin?'

I looked around the room. The adults were sitting on the sofas and chairs, the children on cushions at their feet. Cassie was settling on Clara's lap and Sofa had found a soft knee belonging to P.C Darling's young son.

Pa explained that the children in their Bahá'í Faith community had decided to hold a World Citizenship party to celebrate the oneness of all the world's peoples. Because Bahá'u'lláh's teachings show us how to make the world a better place, the party would begin with some prayers for world peace.

I had had enough listening, but I continued purring and felt it had something to do with the Light of Heaven my mother had taught me about. All I knew was that the feeling of love and kindness in the room was like being part of that Light and it felt very comforting.

I relaxed on Nan's cosy knee and enjoyed the soft music and prayers which both the children and grown ups recited. Afterwards Clara handed everyone a paper leaf and a pencil on which to write their promises of becoming a better World Citizen.

'We need to think of some way we can help serve people and make a solemn promise to do it,' said Drew as he explained the purpose of the tree. 'I'm going to promise to plant trees this year to help make oxygen for us all to breathe,'

'I'm going to write mine as a secret on my leaf,' said Clara, so that everyone will enjoy discovering it when they read the leaves on our World Citizen tree.

'I'm going to promise to keep my room tidy,' said Dillon, a boy with freckles and dimples in his cheeks. His mother chuckled and I wondered why.

'Why don't we all keep our names a secret and write our promises anonymously,' Ma suggested. 'That way only ourselves and God know will know whether we have managed to keep them.'

So it was agreed. The adults were keen to join in too, as long as they did not have to put their names on their leaves. Maya waited for the room to quieten and then she began to read out what was written on each paper leaf, before the children hung each one on the tree of promises.

'This one says, 'I will help my Mum and Dad without expecting extra spending money.

'I will make friends with the boy in the playground at school who is always crying.

'I promise to cheer up my neighbour when he's sad.

'I will stop using insecticide on my garden and find friendlier ways of protecting my plants.

'I will not make unnecessary journeys in my car, but use my bicycle.

'I will try to encourage people instead of getting cross with them.

'I will be careful not to say nasty things about anyone and look at their good qualities instead.'

And so the list of promises went on until all the leaves on the tree had been read out and hung up. My favourite one was, 'I will try to be kind to animals.' That could have been written by any one of the adults or children there. However, I easily guessed who had written the one about knitting blankets for the Cats Protection charity. Nan Knitwarm may be 'doddery on her pins,' but I suspected she could still knit an awesome, cosy cat blanket.

There were some amazing smells coming out of the kitchen, so Ma invited everyone to come and help themselves to the dishes on offer, bringing a tray of food for Nan Knitwarm. I was reluctant to get down from her ample lap, but she reassured me with her twinkly eyes and a mind-message that after she had eaten she would pick me up again.

Cassie fled upstairs, but Sofa sneaked between ankles to beg food from the first person she could lock eyes with. Nan waited until the room had emptied and then set about treating me to a sliver of roast chicken. 'Organic and free range, I believe,' she reassured me.

I wasn't sure what that meant exactly,

but when she said 'free range' she sent me a mind-picture of hens contentedly pecking at the grass in a meadow.

Nan allowed me to lick her plate clean when she thought nobody was looking. 'It will help with the washing up,' she chuckled. Then I settled once more on her warm lap until I heard some strange music playing outside.

My curiosity got the better of me. I made my way to the garden. My tail sailed high as a question mark as I weaved my way in and out of numerous legs and ankles.

The man called Phil was standing on the gravel path with a strange wailing instrument wrapped around his shoulders that he squeezed from time to time. His fingers moved effortlessly over a black and white keyboard. Dragon's eyes bulged in disbelief at the noise it made. I thought he might burst with either indignation or indigestion. But I noticed the smaller children in particular had started to jump up and down in time to the rhythm.

'Circle dancing everyone!' shouted Maya, herding a mixture of eager children and more reluctant adults onto the lawn. Ma explained a few simple steps to everyone and then they were off, whirling around to the wailing music and giggling when they made mistakes. I noticed that someone had moved Nan Knitwarm's chair close to the window so that she could watch everyone. I could see her clapping and smiling in time to the music.

The next moment Thunder was completely unable to resist all those Human Beans and jumped effortlessly over the drystone wall. He landed, would you believe, in the middle of the dancing circle. Everyone fell about laughing. Ma did not bother to tell him off. There were no plants trampled and for once no hosepipe ranged along the garden path.

Now was a good time for me to get up onto that beam in the workshop. I could smell the rain coming closer. Very soon they would have to carry on with the activities indoors.

I was right. A few minutes later the heavens opened and one of those wonderful hilltop cloudbursts spattered on the roof and the Velux windows. I could imagine all the raindrops running down the hillsides and collecting in the tiny brooks and streams, eventually making their way down to the reservoirs and rivers.

Squealing and breathless, the children herded into the workshop to play games and some of the adults who had been dancing decided to go and huddle indoors to dry off by the fire.

Maya seemed to be in charge, while Phil continued to play music on his squeezing instrument. He introduced it as an accordion and showed Drew how to play a chord. A bit loud for my ear comfort, but better than Drew's usual screechy attempts on Pa's guitar.

I soon found out what the bag that looked like a wasp's nest was for. The children had to jump up and bang it with wooden spoons to try to split its sides. When it began to split sweets would fall out. It must have been very tough with several layers of thick paper, because it took ages for it to split right into the centre.

'Wallop! Wallop! Wallop!' went the wooden spoons, as each child jumped up in an attempt to shatter the outer layers. I kept my head well down on the beam so that nobody could see me, or wallop my nose by mistake.

I noticed that Dragon's shoulders seemed to have risen around his ears, or was that my imagination? Then one very eager little chap, who miraculously could jump higher than the taller children, managed to make a serious split in the bag. Sweets began to tumble out and he caught a fistful.

'Well done Mario!' cheered Maya. 'Remember it's a sharing game and because you are the winner you are now in charge of sharing out all the sweets so that everyone gets equal amounts!' I hoped he was good at mathematics.

Phil played a cheerful wiggly tune on his accordion to accompany their eager sharing and shouting. I had never really thought about sharing before. Spud had often shared his leftovers and more importantly Chip had shared a good deal of his time with me. Maybe as the oldest cat in the family I needed to teach Cassandra and Sofa about sharing; especially when it came to sharing the heat from the fire on a cold evening.

When the children began to tire of their games and creep indoors to get more food and drink, I decided to risk following them to find Nan Knitwarm's knee again. She would be wondering where I had disappeared to?

'I believe you made an arrest, P.C Darling?' Nan croaked in a tired voice. 'All down to Drew and Clara being so observant.'

I rubbed against her swollen ankles and she patted her knee in her usual way to give me permission to jump up.

'Indeed! If it hadn't been for them we'd never have discovered who was stealing all the capstones off the stone walling. It was a young fella called

Newton,' the policeman replied.

Nan choked on a large piece of chocolate cake that she was trying to inch between her false teeth. 'That sounds like my nephew Newton,' she spluttered indignantly. 'I bet he dumped Tigger on the moors because he could not be bothered to feed him whilst I was in hospital!'

'Well, he will be up before the magistrate pretty soon. Perhaps he'll not be sent to prison. As this was his first offence, maybe he will have to do a course in rebuilding drystone walls as a punishment. My guess is that he'll have to repair all the ones he's damaged.'

'Wow! That would be really fair,' Drew exclaimed as he pounced on Sofa before she could attack P.C Darling's shoelaces. (When you are feeling lazy and comfortable, there is no better way of getting things done than sending Human Beans a mind-message. Well done, Drew! He was learning to pick up mind-messages very efficiently.)

'We also found a stash of stolen

jewellery in his flat. We are investigating whose it might be.'

Nan seemed to choke for a minute, as the chocolate cake, having an amazing mind of its own, began a free fall into her lavender hankie along with the lower set of her false teeth. 'No need for shat, P.She. Darling! I shushpect he was looking after it for me whilsht I was in hoshpital!' she coughed and spluttered again. 'However, ish would be really wonderful if he could do a courshe in dryshtone walling. He would be able to get a deshcent job with a shkill like that. Shet him on his feet it would!' She fumbled about a bit and managed to get her bottom teeth back in with a click and a snap.

I wondered why Nan was sticking up for her nephew when he had been so cruel, dishonest and destructive. Maybe she was one of those rare Human Beans who always wanted to give someone a second chance.

The party had been a busy and happy day. We had helped tidy up of course, finishing off the leftovers and chasing the streamers as they were being pulled down. I had a very warm feeling inside. I knew I would see Nan Knitwarm and share her lap once more.

After all the visitors had helped clear up and wended their way home, we all sat exhausted around the fire in the sitting room.... four Human Beans, three felines and a World Citizen tree full of leafy promises and decorations picturing smiling faces in all different skin tones and headgear.

'If you could write a promise to hang on the tree, Sofa and Cassie, what would it be?' I mind-messaged to my sisters.

They both thought very hard for a moment and then Sofa whispered in a slightly less confident voice than usual, 'I promise to try to be a much better sister.'

'Me too,' prrped Cassie. 'We were so suspicious and horrible towards you when you first came and you have never done anything to harm us.'

'What would your promise be, Tigger Digger?' asked Sofa.

'I think it would be a strong wish of well-being and peace to all my friends, my family and my enemies.... even to Bumfleas, Glumteaser, Gobblechops, Yarlminger and Clawit. They did not know any better,' I yawned. 'They had no real family to show them warmth and affection.... No one to feed them if they were hungry. I wish, I wish....' But I never did finish what I'd been trying to say. Everyone including me had nodded off to sleep.

EPILOGUE

The fortnightly 'adopt a granny' times with my former owner seemed to come around surprisingly quickly. The children called her 'Nan' of course and I had to share her lap with Cassie and Sofa, taking it in turns. After all, I was there to set them an example. Pa called it 'being a good role model.' I wondered why Sofa rolled about so much. Maybe she was trying to be a good roll model herself and Pa just could not spell!

I had to be prepared to share my favourite Human Bean, but I noticed that Sofa was now quite happy to lay her head on one of Nan's knees and allow me to put my head on the other.... no hissing either, just the odd lick of my nose or paw. It was all very comforting. I knew it would take a while for Cassandra to be equally relaxed around me, but it would happen. I had saved her from drowning after all.

'Do cats really have nine lives, Nan?' asked Clara one afternoon after we had all eaten a particularly large Sunday lunch. I was lying on my back with my white tummy exposed for Clara to rub, but now my ears pricked up. I had spent so many lives lately I had lost count.

'Well you know, that is just a saying.... what is called 'an old wives' tale'. Because cats are so curious, they are always getting into one type of danger or another. Tigger Digger must easily have spent nine lives when he was just a young kitten. There was the time he got accidently locked in a garden shed when a neighbour went on holiday; the time he sniffed inside a coal bunker and its lid fell down on him, trapping him inside with just his tail peeking out; the time my neighbour's vicious Jack Russell chased him so far up a tree, he couldn't get down. Then there was the time his flea collar got caught on a branch and he almost choked. Never wore a collar after that.

'Once, he even set his tail on fire from sleeping too close to the fire and I nearly called out the fire brigade, before I found the awful smell was his tail singeing. It was one scrape after another. He always had to sniff everything out to investigate in a truly detective way. I really should have named him 'Sherlock Holmes',' she chuckled.

So Nan calculated that I had already spent nine lives even before I was dumped on the moors. It wasn't true then. Cats could have many more than nine lives. Phew! What a relief. Maybe I would not be taken to the Light of Heaven quite as soon as I thought.

'How are you getting along with your new neighbours?' asked Nan. 'Have they settled into Chip and Spud's farm?'

'Fine,' said Drew. 'We often stop and play with their sheepdog when the school bus drops us off at the crossroads. He's not chained up, but he knows not to go far from the farmhouse he's guarding. He always drops a frisby at our feet for us to throw for him,' said Drew, who had always secretly wanted a dog.

'The farmer's wife's called Mrs. Penstemon. Ma and Pa introduced us when we took them some apple pie. She let us into the barn to see some kittens that had been born. They're so sweet.... Only a few weeks old. She says she is going to feed all the wild cats now. She's trying to tame them. She says there is no need for them to be so vicious if they are not half starving.'

I was so relieved to hear that from Clara. I am glad my wish has partially come true. The thought of other animals being unhappy when I am SO happy is quite uncomfortable. If the Wild Bunch comes to know constant kindness, then there is hope they will eventually change for the better.

'How is Newton? Did he have to go to prison?' queried Clara.

'No, thank goodness. He was told he

must take a course in drystone walling and then he had to repair all the walls he'd helped ruin. You should see the muscles on him now. He's really fit and strong from all that work.'

I wasn't so keen to revisit my acquaintance with Newton, especially if he was stronger than ever.

'He's quite a changed character. Now he has a special skill, he's found work and some self-respect. He's getting some help with his gambling problem and learning how to manage money. He's returned all my jewellery, even the watch he had pawned. More importantly, he visits me quite often to tell me all about his work and his new friends.'

Nan smiled in satisfaction. She had really helped her nephew to turn around his life by giving him a second chance.

A few weekends later he even drove Nan over to see our whole family. I was satisfied to note that his outer gleam around his bean shape was much kinder... more mellow. Although I could still detect a whiff of black pudding and stale sausage, he smelled much nicer, too. He seemed to hang his head in a peculiar way when he was introduced to Ma and Pa. Maybe he was ashamed of all the trouble he had caused. I noticed he had a different car, an estate car. I thought I had better note the registration number just in case. It was GLOW 954Z.

I mind-messaged it to Drew and Clara. Message received.

DISCUSSION QUESTIONS

Often children can get so much more out of a book if we read it alongside them. Here are some suggested questions a parent or teacher might like to explore when coming to the end of each chapter. Maybe it will help with the building of vocabulary, with the understanding of human emotions, or even assist in building relationships. There are, of course, no right and wrong answers.... only the subtle development of seeing things from different angles. The children themselves will have even more interesting questions, I am sure.

CHAPTER 1
THE BAGGED PUSS

a) Who was being cruel to Tigger Digger in this first chapter? How do you think they were being cruel?

b) Is it alright to be cruel to animals sometimes?

c) What has made Tigger worried or frightened in the story so far?

d) Is calling someone by a nickname such as 'Noddle' being useful or kind?

e) Which creatures have been kind and helpful to Tigger in this chapter?

f) Why does Tigger call human beings 'Human Beans?'

g) What does Tigger think Human Beans call sending and receiving mind-messages? Do you ever receive or send mind-messages?

CHAPTER 2
TRAPPED

a) In what ways did Nan Knitwarm and Farmer Parkin show they cared for their animals? What is the difference between a farm animal and a pet?

b) Which creatures show they are brave and courageous and able to step over their fear?

c) Why do you think Tigger is prejudiced against children? What does 'prejudice' mean?

d) Are you suspicious of Newton? What do you think he is planning to do by spying on Bimblewick House with his binoculars?

CHAPTER 3
DRIVEN AWAY

a) Is there any way you feel sorry for the Wild Bunch of feral cats living in the farm barn?

b) Are the Wild Bunch really tough and courageous?

c) Why do the wild cats treat Tigger so cruelly? What are they frightened about?

d) Have you ever been bullied and, if so, what did you do about it?

e) Why does Farmer Parkin get so angry with the Wild Bunch?

f) Lord Bimblewick loves his old cars and takes great care of them. Tigger is surprised that Human Beans are so attached to their possessions. Do you think being possessive of the things we own is a good thing?

CHAPTER 4
TRACKED

a) What sort of friend is Chip? Is he a fair weather friend? How does he show his loyalty to Tigger?

b) Is Tigger a coward, or do you think he was wise to avoid the wild cats at the farm when they started to gang up on him? Is it sometimes better to be wise than brave and courageous?

c) TLC is short for, or is an acronym for 'Tender, Loving Care.' How is this shown to Tigger?

d) Why do you think Chip had a prejudice and fear of people who wear Wellington boots? How was he able to conquer this fear?

e) What should Tigger do to overcome his fear of and prejudice against children? Is it true that children are always cruel to animals?

f) Chip and Tigger have a conversation about paying back kindness which mentions paying it forward instead. Can you think of any real examples where this sort of behaviour of paying it back or forwards has happened?

CHAPTER 5
HOUNDED

a) Have you ever felt sad because

someone you were fond of has gone to live far away? What helped you to recover from this sadness?

b) What advice would you give to Tigger now that his two best friends have moved far away?

c) There seem to be all sorts of people in the world who have different good and bad qualities and virtues. Do people have to be perfect to be kind?

d) Why does Tigger not think it would be a good idea to beg a home from the Bimblewicks or the Thwackits?

e) In what ways is Tigger helped to get down off the roof-ridge at the Bimblewicks' barn?

CHAPTER 6
GROUNDED

a) How does Tigger reassure the hedgehog he means him no harm?

b) Why is Tigger unsure whether Dragon is real or not?

c) What is the difference between a wish and a prayer? Do they sometimes come true?

d) What are the little things that Clara and Drew do to enable Tigger to overcome his prejudice and fear of children?

e) Why does Ma initially keep the kittens away from Tigger Digger?

CHAPTER 7
MAYHEM

a) Clara and Drew knew they should not be letting Tigger in through Drew's bedroom window without permission from Ma and Pa. Why did they keep it a secret and why did they find keeping the secret so exciting?

b) How did telling a lie to his mum make Drew feel? Is it always important to tell the truth?

c) Why do you think the Smith family forgive Tigger for taking them a present of a dead rabbit?

d) Is it always good to forgive people if they behave unwisely or do wrong things?

CHAPTER 8
BONDING

a) We all seem to have a lower nature and a higher nature. Tigger is very tempted to follow his instinct and chase the vole he has caught. Drew tells him to drop it and he obeys. Do you think there are times when people should obey God's laws and advice and ignore what their Lower Self is telling them to do? Can you think of examples?

b) Why do you think that Tigger feels belonging to a family is very special?

c) Because he is older and more experienced than Sofa and Cassandra, Tigger feels he should be a good role model and set the kittens a good example. Who, or what has taught this wisdom to Tigger?

d) 'Everything we do has consequences,' says Tigger to Sofa when she runs dangerously between the wheels of a truck. Can you think of things that you have done which have had either good or bad results?

e) What did Tigger and Sofa manage to achieve together by doing some serious teamwork?

CHAPTER 9
THE PARTY

a) What did Tigger enjoy about the Bahá'í nineteen day feast at the cottage?

b) Tigger thought that it might be a good idea to include the kittens in more decision-making next time all three of them were consulting together. His instinct told him it would help them become wiser. What do you think youngsters are practising when they are allowed to join in adult discussions?

c) Do people from Bahá'í religious communities all over the world always celebrate in the same way, or do you think it is up to the local community to decide for itself at the nineteen day feast?

d) Pa explains at the beginning of the World Citizenship party that they are celebrating the oneness of humankind and the teachings Bahá'u'lláh has brought for a better world. What do you think some of those teachings might be?

e) If you were going to make a World Citizenship promise, what would yours be?

f) How and why did Nan Knitwarm help her nephew, Newton?

g) Do you think that Tigger Digger was wise or realistic by not entirely trusting the 'new' Newton?

If you have enjoyed discussing these questions with young readers you might find the following book and website very useful:

'THE FAMILY VIRTUES GUIDE - Simple Ways to Bring Out the best in Our Children and Ourselves'

by Linda Kavelin Popov, with Dan Popov, Ph.D. and John Kavelin.

https://virtuesproject.com

AUTHOR'S NOTES

This story has been a lifetime in the making, because it is full of true-life tales about all the nine cats we have homed. Most of the incidents involving the misadventures of Tigger happened for real. They are, however, embellished by the characters of imagined 'Human Beans'.

The mind-message or mind picture process was taught to me by Lucy, our beloved tortoiseshell cat, who became blind and deaf during her latter years, but whom I found I could summon by sending her a mind picture. If I needed her to take away my pain when I was bedridden, I had only to send her an image of her jumping on the bed and settling down against my spine and within a minute she would be there, doing exactly that. I found the process came in very handy too when I needed a specific 'Human Bean' to telephone us.

Sooty was an inscrutable black cat with a smudge of grey on his chest. He was with us for nineteen long years. He survived running between the wheels of a truck as a kitten, but was obviously good at learning from his mistakes. He was the cat whom we taught to bring us beautiful live 'presents' instead of very dead ones. Unfortunately we did not succeed in training any of the others in that respect; so there was always something for the crow and magpie larder. He makes his first appearance in one of my adult novels 'Where Rowans Intertwine' as the inscrutable priestess's cat, Mwg.

We abandoned the use of flea collars and name collars for our cats when one of them was found suspended from a tree by his neck. We were in time to save him, but it taught us a lesson.

The incident in the stream is a memory of when my dog helped me save the life of his puppy by pulling him from a rushing river. I got very wet and muddy that day, but was compensated by meeting my husband, Gordon, properly for the first time. So many memories and so much fun!

The real Tigger did have a horribly tough time settling in with our two Cats Protection rescue kittens, Sophie and Cassie. When we found him, emaciated and flea ridden outside our kitchen door, it was obvious he had been dumped on the moors and had been living rough for several months.

He was very wise and submitted to the kittens in a very gentle way until they could completely trust him. It took a few months and lots of hissing, using the circular table as a roundabout in the glazed porch.

The idea of Liberace came about when a stray peacock decided to roost in the bluebell wood down our lane. Every day he would call at each cottage up the lane for a snack, but I think he liked our cat food the best. He was happily rehomed by a neighbour - (a mile or so away in rural Anglesey) - who had a peahen. I'm glad to say he established his own family.

Our family all agree that out of our many pets, Tigger Digger has been the gentlest and most affectionate. (That was after we taught him that we were not attacking him if we tickled his tantalising white, furry tum of course.)

So thank you to Smudge, Samantha, Leo, Sooty, Lucy, Smokey, Cassandra, Sophie and Tiggy for all the TLC and adventurous entertainment you have given our Bahá'í family over the years. We are grateful for your toleration of all the nineteen-day feasts; for dodging feet on holy day celebrations; for providing comfort on laps for refugees and house guests; and for just being feline.

This book would never have been published if it were not for the help of my family. Thank you to husband Gordon for the lively illustrations, the photograph of the South Yorkshire Moors on the jacket, and for all the patient proofreading.

Thanks to our lovely son and daughter, Andy and Claire, for all their timely, wise suggestions after reading the first rough draft and for befriending the many cats who make up this story.

Thanks to Kertu Laur from Sarafista Designs for composition of the attractive book jacket: www.sarafista.com and to Yvonne Betancourt's for her excellent work on the formatting of both the paperback and ebook: www.ebook-format.com

Thanks go to Adobe Stock for providing a virtual look-alike image of Tigger for the jacket.

Grateful appreciation for advice and printing of the paperback for book signings goes to Steve Plummer, Business and Development Manager at Ruddocks Integrated Design and Print Agency, Lincoln. https://www.ruddocks.co.uk

For more information about the teachings of the Bahá'í Faith please go to www.bahai.org